CALEB, MY SON

CALEB,
MY SON

A Novel by
LUCY DANIELS

AN AUTHORS GUILD BACKINPRINT.COM EDITION

AN AUTHORS GUILD BACKINPRINT.COM EDITION

Published by iUniverse.com, Inc.

For information address:
iUniverse.com, Inc.
5220 S 16th, Ste. 200
Lincoln, NE 68512
www.iuniverse.com

Originally published by J.B. Lippincott Co.

ISBN: 0-595-19892-9

Printed in the United States of America

CHAPTER

1

ASA was at work at the time of the accident; it was three o'clock in the afternoon. He had just finished washing the car—a black Buick—which was parked just outside the garage in the widest part of the gravel driveway so that the sun brought out its highlights. As yet, however, the finish was not very shiny; Asa had only begun to apply the wax. He was up on the old kitchen stool, smearing it over the top when the girl, Lola, came for him.

She was a plump, black little girl from the other side of town. She had only been working for the Lawrences since Ellen had quit to have her baby, and, though that was nearly two years ago now, Asa still did not know her very well. He did not know her because he did not care to know her; he did not care to know anyone from the other side of town. He remembered, as he watched her scuffle towards the car through the cloud of dust raised by her dirty sandals, that that was where all the trouble came from—the other side of town. His lips protruded with discontent. Besides it annoyed him to be interrupted.

"Asa . . ." she whined. "Asa?"

"What?"

"Miss 'Liz'beth say to tell you telephone."

"Huh!" He stopped rubbing and leaned over to get a better glimpse of her face.

"Telephone. . . . Somebody want you on de telephone."

Then he was really angry. He climbed down, slapped his rag against the hood of the car, and started out across the sun-white gravel to the back porch. The screen door slammed behind him, and old fat Martha looked up from the dough she was kneading. "What's eatin' you, man?" she asked. But Asa did not answer. The very knowledge that she expected one made him tired, and besides he was too busy trying to think of a good way to tell May off. He could hear her voice even before he got to the phone— "Papa, please couldn' you pick me up t'night? . . . I had t' spend the bus money Mama give me. I had t' have that movie magazine. . . . An', Papa . . . I'm so tihad; I'm plumb wo' out. They jest workin' me t' death."

Prickles of perspiration popped out all over Asa's face. He would really give it to her this time; he would really let her have it. At eighteen she was plenty old enough to learn a little self-reliance. He would just say, "Walk home then. If you ain't got the money, walk home." And after last night too! The anger put a sour taste in his mouth. After he had laid down the law about them phoning him at work all the time. Maybe Miss 'Liz'beth and Mr. Charles didn't ever say anything, but it still wasn't proper. He had told them they must never do it again except in the case of an emergency. He picked up the receiver and listened for a moment to be sure no one was on the phone upstairs. "Hello," he snapped. "Well, wha' d' you want?"

But it was not May who answered; it was Effie. Her soft, usually impassive voice seemed to tremble over the wire. "Asa, I'm sorry t' call you theah. . . . I . . . But . . . Asa can you come home?"

"Wha'sa mattah, Effie? . . . You sick?" But he knew before he asked that she was not. Effie would never have called him for that reason. As his wife, she considered it just as much her duty to obey him as to love him; sometimes she carried that obedience to extremes. Had she considered herself sick enough to call, she would not have been able to hold the receiver.

"No, I'm not sick. . . . They's been an accident down t' that house they buildin'. The whole top fell in, an' Ellen's Joe—he were up theah. They didn' even get 'im t' the hospital. . . . Couldn' y' come home, Asa? I'm scahed. You should see Ellen—an' only two months t' go."

By the sound of her voice, Asa knew her soft puffy face must be all pinched in with its effort to keep back the tears. "Yeah," he said. "I'll be home. I'll ask Miss 'Liz'beth right now. Wheah you goin'? Home o' to Ellen's?"

"Home."

"Okay, I'll be right theah." He put the receiver back into place, hesitated for a moment beside the phone, and then went to look for Miss 'Liz'beth.

She was upstairs in the room Mr. Charles used for a study. She was seated at the small table beneath the window, sorting through a shoe box of cards. She turned in her chair when he stopped in the doorway.

" 'Scuse me, Miss 'Liz'beth," he began. He looked down at his feet as he always did when her eyes were on him. "But is it all right if I leave soon's I finish the car? We got a little trouble t' home."

He looked up at her then to see if she was annoyed. But her round, calm face did not move a muscle; her transparent blue eyes betrayed no emotion whatsoever. "Oh, I'm sorry," she said. "Is somebody ill?" Her voice, as always, was cool and charming. Even to me, Asa thought, a perfect lady. And kind too, always kind, he reminded himself. He had been a fool to think she might be angry.

"No'm, not sick. . . . But Joe—my Ellen's husband—he was killed at work t'day. An', you know, Ma'm, Ellen's 'spectin' a baby."

Her face still showed nothing, and her finger did not stray

from the place it was holding in the shoe box of cards. But her voice was soft and sympathetic. "Oh, how very sad!" she sighed. "You go home right now, Asa. Don't bother with the car; leave it for Henry—unless you need him home too."

"No'm, jest me. . . . Effie needs me."

"Well, go right ahead then. . . . With Mr. Charles away, it's not so necessary for you to be here anyhow. But I hope you'll be back by Saturday. You know, we're having that dinner party Saturday night."

He assured her that he would be back long before Saturday —probably the very next day. Then he hurried down the stairs and out through the kitchen again. Martha stopped him there. Though a good woman, Martha always had to have a story. When she didn't have one, she invented one; she made it her business to know everything about everybody. She lived only three blocks from the large, white frame house where Effie and Asa and five of the young Blakes lived. Therefore, in order to have even the least bit of privacy, Asa had long ago learned to talk to her about nothing except the weather. Now she asked, "Where you goin', Asa? Can't be t' work, not that fast."

"Home."

"Home? This time o' day? Ain't mo' than two-thirty, an' that car all smeared wid wax. You tell Miss 'Liz'beth?"

"Yeah, I tol' her."

"Wha'sa mattah? . . . Somebody sick?"

"No, they was a accident ovah t' that house they buildin' on Martin Street. Whole top fell in. An' Joe . . . Ellen's Joe . . . he was up theah."

Martha put down the jelly glass with which she had been cutting biscuits; she put both floury hands on her hips. "How bad he hurt?" She pushed him further, though the answer was obvious even before she asked.

"He was killed."

"Lawd! Lawd!" she gasped in the stricken tone she used

for all disasters large or small. "Po' li'l Ellen! Her time 'most up too. An' that otha li'l one allus undah foot." She rolled her big black eyes. "Anybody else hurt?"

That was what she really wanted to know—all the bloody details—but Asa did not wait to tell her. Before the words were well out of her mouth, the screen door had banged shut and he was behind the wheel of the old Ford Mr. Charles had given him.

The car started violently and crunched over the gravel. But at the foot of the hill Asa slowed it to a stop. He wanted to tell Henry the news before Martha did; besides he wanted to tell him about polishing the car. Henry looked up when he heard the tires on the gravel. He saw his father open the front door, and so, putting down his hoe, he went to meet him.

Henry was not tall, and his small frame was a little too sparsely covered with flesh. His face—open and unemotional —revealed his whole personality. Henry had an older brother, Caleb, who was tall and handsome; whose face was quick and eager; who incited great love—and great hatred— in others. Caleb was the image of all his father's hopes and dreams. But still he lacked Henry's placid stability; and Asa valued that highly. He found a great comfort in Henry. He was a boy to be depended upon, one who would follow —unquestioning—in his father's footsteps and who possessed, despite his stature, the great strength of endurance.

He did not call out now, but came within a few yards of his father before he spoke. "What is it, Pa?"

"Miss 'Liz'beth wants you t' come finish waxin' the car. I'm goin' home."

"You sick?"

"No. . . . That's what I come t' tell ye. . . . Joe was kilt. The roof o' that house they buildin' on Martin Street fell in."

"Lawd!" The boy's eyeballs rolled almost completely out of sight, and his face grew thinner than ever.

"I'm goin' home t' see— You won' fo'git the car," his father continued, changing to a more businesslike tone.

"No, Pa."

Asa hurried back to the Ford.

Cameron Street seemed morbidly silent in the early afternoon sun. The only visible sign of life was the wash hung out to dry. And even that did not seem very much alive. For there was no breeze to set it flopping; the sheets, the shirts, the faded overalls sagged like the dank ghosts of a forgotten race of men. The old tar road had grown gray in spots, and any car driving over it—especially Asa's rickety one—shook violently in protest against the bumps and dents.

Asa rarely thought about the road or even about the tired, grimy appearance of the neighborhood. That was because he rarely came home at two-thirty in the afternoon. Normally it was at least six o'clock and sometimes after eight before he got there. Then children were running up and down, calling one another, playing hide and seek or crack the whip. Their fathers came trudging slowly homeward in ragged overalls and with rusty metal lunch boxes clanging under their arms. The smell of roasting pork and boiling greens filled the air. And usually Effie—as soon as she heard the car in the street—hurried out to meet him.

This afternoon, however, the street was dead. The children were either taking naps or still in school. The women were inside, cooking or washing or stealing a snooze. Even the trees in yards here and there—chestnuts, sycamores, his own prize pecan—seemed forlorn under the gaudy glare of the afternoon sun. And though, thanks to the rain of the night before, some of the dusty, gray dryness had disappeared, the muddy red ruts in most of the yards were even more depressing.

Asa pulled the car up to the curb and got out. He stopped for a moment, hands in pockets, and scanned the "lawn" in front of his well-kept but ancient white frame house. He wondered if after all the work he and the boys had put into it they would at last be able to grow grass in this stubborn clay. He doubted that; it would have been completely against the usual course of things. He reminded himself also that he must check the cost if they were to paint the house that summer.

But these thoughts were only momentary. Before even one of his curious neighbors had reached her front door at the sound of a car at this hour of the day, Asa had gone up the jagged cement path to the door. Usually if Effie did not meet him at the curb, he called her name when he got inside. This day he did not. He shut the screen door carefully behind him and tiptoed from one dark room to another. He remembered doing the same thing as a boy the summer his mother and her new baby died of diphtheria, and even after all those years the memory brought a kind of panic.

Effie, having heard the car, met him in the doorway of the kitchen. Though not tall, she was a heavy woman. Her body through years of black-eyed peas and fat back had become wide and shapeless. Yet the impression she made was not that of a fat person; most people—especially those closest to her—saw only a bundle of sweet, comfortable curves. This afternoon her black eyes were dilated with anxiety. But aside from that and the way her whispered words jerked out, she seemed perfectly calm. Effie was always like that, Asa reminded himself—even that Sunday when the church had burned right next door.

"Asa," she began, grasping one of his large hard hands. "She scares me, Asa. She ain't cried one single tear. . . . Evah since I brung 'er home—all aftahnoon she jest sets theah sewin' on that dress fo' the li'l girl. . . . Asa, it ain't right fo' a girl not t' cry."

He squeezed the helpless pudgy hands. "No, Effie, it ain't. I'll speak to 'er. . . . Wheah's the chile?"

"Dora? I put 'er t' bed fo' a nap. . . . You speak t' Ellen, Asa. She always close t' you." Effie walked past him toward the rickety white staircase. She was trying, Asa knew, to leave him alone with Ellen; he obediently went into the kitchen.

Ellen was seated in the back doorway, hemming a light blue dress. Her hair was pulled back severely into a knot at the nape of her neck. Below it five little knobs of vertebrae formed stepping stones to the scoop neck of her dress. Her thin brown hands moved nimbly in the flickering sunlight.

"Ellen, honey," Asa began softly. At the sound of his voice, tiny hard cords formed in her back, extending outward from the little knobs. Though her eyes remained intently fixed on the work in her lap, her fingers ceased to move.

Asa put his hand on her head as he had done often when she was a little girl, when there were crinkly little pigtails on it instead of this sleekness like a horse's mane. He hated to see his children hurt. It happened time and time again, but he had not yet learned that he could not save them. He still longed to bear their pain; it would have been easier that way.

Now, faced with the grief of his oldest daughter, he could only try to say the most comforting thing. "Don' worry, Ellen chile," he whispered. "Mama an' I take care o' you an' the chile. . . . You know, Ellen, mebbe it's bettah you cry."

But he knew as the words left his mouth that it was foolish. Ellen never cried unless she was angry. It was her way just as the other children had their ways—just as Liza, solemn as she was, could sparkle with humor; just as May was forever either laughing or crying; just as Saul liked to sit on the front steps and stare into space. This was Ellen's way. He remembered the time her puppy ran out in front of a car. They had all cried—he and the children on the street. But

Ellen had not shed a tear. She had just carefully wrapped the mutilated little body in an old towel and dug a hole for it in the back yard.

Ellen looked up at him now with a thin face as smooth as her mother's except for the little pucker between her sparse eyebrows. "I know, Pa. I know," she said. "But sometimes you jest cain't cry." She folded her work impatiently and stood up. Asa was surprised to see how full her body had become; this evidence of growing life within her brought warm moisture to his eyes.

As if reading his mind, she placed one hand on her bulging stomach. "But I ain't sorry 'bout the baby," she said. "Maybe it'll be a boy. . . . Maybe it'll be a boy an' I kin call 'im Joseph." After that Asa could not speak at all. He watched in silence as she walked slowly up and down the room and finally sat down again to continue her sewing. Once again he was forced to accept his helplessness.

CHAPTER

2

THE boss man at Wilson Builders Inc. was tall and heavy. He had a red face, and when he talked too much he ran out of breath. His thin white hair was combed carefully over his bald spots. His suit was a double-breasted one of light gray material. He looked comfortable and very prosperous behind his desk in the air-conditioned office.

It was three-thirty the same afternoon, and Asa had come to tend to Ellen's money matters. He hated doing it; he looked tensely down at his shoes when the secretary showed him in. Still it was his duty, and he knew the longer he waited the harder it would be.

The boss man—Mr. Cronin—motioned to a chair before the desk, and Asa sat down. "Well, Blake," the red-faced man began. "I understand you're the father-in-law of Joe Marsh. . . . His death was tragic—especially since, they tell me, his wife is expecting a second child."

"Yes suh," Asa said to fill in the gap. He could feel his throat tightening, and he remembered what his son, Caleb, always said about not letting white folks walk all over you. Caleb was one of the main reasons for his coming here, and, remembering that, he made up his mind to speak up before he lost his nerve. "Mistah Cronin, suh," he began, forcing himself to look straight into the pale blue eyes. "That's what I come t' talk about. . . . Joe . . . he been workin' heah

a good while—goin' on seven yeahs now. . . . Mistah Cronin
. . . I wondah . . . Do . . . I mean, jes' how much do Ellen
get?"

The eyes bulged in the beefsteak face. "Oh, you needn't
worry, Blake. . . . Wilson Incorporated always pays the
funeral expenses."

"Yes suh, but—" Asa faltered again, suddenly frozen by
the cruel icy eyes. "Yes suh, but what about insurance o'
somethin' like that. Joe was always tellin' me 'bout all the
things they took out o' his pay check."

"Y-yes? . . . Perhaps you misunderstood. . . . We only
pay the funeral expenses. You see, Joe worked only six years
for us."

"Yeah, but what about his wife an' the chi'ren?" Asa saw
the white man's hand reach under the desk for something.
For a cigar, he thought, until the hand emerged still empty.
Then he realized that the secretary was standing behind him.

"Mr. Rogers has been waiting ten minutes to see you,
sir," she said.

"Thank you, Miss Evans." The secretary turned again and
shut the door behind her. Mr. Cronin stood up. "Well, I'm
sorry, Blake," he said in the prosperous voice of a merchant
who knows he has the upper hand. "I'm afraid that's all I
can do. . . . I'd like to do more; I always would, but my
hands are tied. I'm sure you understand. . . . Now, if you'll
excuse me, I have a client; he's been waiting some time."

The two of them by that time were standing beside the
door. Asa fumbled with his hat, uncertain as to what to
do or say. Finally he muttered, "Thank you, suh," and
ducked out the frosted-glass door.

He had not, after all, really expected to gain anything by
that visit. He had only made it to pacify Caleb and as a
stab in the dark because he knew every extra penny would
be a help. Perhaps, despite what he had said, Mr. Cronin
would still give Ellen something. White folks were like that

sometimes. Then, too, if worse came to worse, he could go to Mr. Charles. There was always Mr. Charles.

His next visit was to Winbourne's Funeral Home. He hated going there. A white man owned it, but the men inside were all black, and the business was wholly with Negroes. That, however, did nothing to improve the atmosphere. The clerks, though colored, were like no people Asa had ever known. Their hair was dekinked and plastered. They wore shiny black business suits—twice as neat and twice as hard-looking as any Asa had seen on white men. Their voices, though soft, were sharp and painfully cool.

He told them who he was, and they led him into the back to see what they had done with Joe. They seemed proud of their work, but Asa hardly looked. He just glanced at the pine box and told them he was sure it was all going to be fine. Then, just to be sure Mr. Cronin had not fooled him, he asked how much it would cost.

"Oh, Mr. Blake," the sugar-coated voice told him, "you are not to concern yourself. The company is looking after that."

Caleb was late coming home for supper that evening. Had he thought about it he would have remembered how it bothered the family when he was late. But Caleb rarely stopped to think about anything like that. His mind was too full of other, more important matters; he did not have time.

He was a tall boy. At twenty-two, though his face was soft and young—almost boyish, the thick, bulging muscles in his shoulders and back seemed to emanate power. Women who did not know him could not keep their eyes from trailing him down a street; men who did know him never quarreled with Caleb Blake.

This evening especially they knew enough to avoid him. True, he had been reasonably civil to those daring enough to whisper him the news of Joe's death. But they had moved away immediately; for, the anger, though restrained, had been quite evident. Caleb kicked stones in the road; he flung aside branches of shrubbery; he growled and jerked away from a little boy who caught hold of his pants leg.

With each step anger gripped his mind more tightly. He was remembering the talk he had had with Joe less than a week ago. They had been sitting on the front steps, Joe humped over with his elbows on his knees, smoking a cigarette. Naturally, because Joe was the foreman in charge, they had talked about the Martin Street house, and Joe had said he didn't like the job at all. He had said the boss was refusing them the additional temporary supports they needed so that there was the constant risk of somebody getting hurt.

Caleb had always hated injustice; now his mind screamed out against it. "God damn that boss man," it shrieked. "The dirty, lousy murderer! God damn him!" His fury was so overpowering that he did not realize he had turned into Cameron Street. He was surprised when Saul came running out to meet him, and for a few minutes he did not even see that his whole family was sitting on the porch waiting for him.

They had been there a long time—each occupied with something but also hungry for the evening meal at which Effie liked to have the whole family present. An old alarm clock looked out on the porch from the parlor window sill, and Effie had been watching it ever since quarter past five. Every few minutes she announced to no one in particular, "Caleb's late."

But no one answered her; they knew she did not expect an answer. May went on applying the shiny pink enamel to her nails. Ellen cuddled little Dora on the hammock. Saul and Henry intently pursued their checker game on the front steps. Only Asa and Liza, who was correcting her school papers, even raised their eyes to glance at the street.

Before long, however, Saul asked, "Mama, when we gonna eat?"

"If Caleb ain't home by six-thirty, we eat widout 'im."

"I cain't wait no latah, Mama. I got a date fo' seven-thirty, an' I wanta dress afta suppah. I don' wanta be all hot an' smelly." May put the top back on the bottle of nail polish and held her fingers out to dry. "You know, Liza," she went on, "you should see some o' them white ladies comes t' get fixed up. An'—cou'se I don' get none bein' jest 'girl Friday'—but you oughta see them tips. Twenty-five—" But nobody listened; they had heard it a million times before. For May was always like that—either conspicuously sulking in a corner or talking, talking, talking without so much as time out to breathe. After she had told you about her day at the beauty parlor, she went on to the boy she was dating that night, then to a story she had read in a movie magazine, and finally back to the beauty parlor again.

Yet Henry, who had double-dated with her once, had come home with a strange story of his sister's silence. The whole family had found it difficult to believe, but inside they had always known there must be some secret like that, something to make the boys keep coming. For, besides being a jabber-box, May was not pretty—not half as pretty as either of her sisters. Though tall, she looked younger than her eighteen years. Her skin was too light—almost yellow, and every bone in her body stuck out—especially her ugly, bird-like elbows. That was because—as they were forever telling her—she never took time to eat properly. She was always in too much of a hurry for breakfast and supper, and no matter what you told her, she still spent her lunch money on toilet water and movie magazines.

Finally May went in to press her dress, but the rest of them still sat there in silence. Effie shelled her black-eyed peas; the checker game on the steps progressed; Dora piped on in her lisping monologue. Asa, his wicker chair propped at an angle against the porch railing, smoked his pipe and surveyed his family. He found it pleasant to do that. It brought him a sense of peace, but at the same time—and he could not understand this—there was a tinge of sadness too.

It was natural, of course, to feel that way about Ellen. But those feelings were even more poignant when his eyes fell on Liza bent over her papers. She was the prettiest of them all. Her skin was very dark—almost black, and her hair—though not as smooth as Ellen's—was pulled back into the same kind of knot at the nape of her neck. Also, like Ellen, she was tall and slender, but she had some of May's sparkle too. Her face was smooth and serene, yet at the same time exciting, and there was a glint in her black eyes, a sort of fire behind her broad, white-toothed smile. It often seemed to Asa that she of all his children had the greatest capacity for warmth. Yet she had never been out with men; she was quiet—sometimes too quiet. And now that she had graduated from college—a feat which no other Blake had ever accomplished—she devoted her whole life to teaching fifth grade. Here again was pain for Asa. Here again he longed to help his child and could not.

"When we gonna eat, Mama?" The checker game was over, and Saul no longer had anything to divert him.

Effie glanced at the clock again. It said six twenty-five. "Ten mo' minutes," she said. "Jes' wait ten mo' minutes. If he ain't heah then, we'll eat widout him."

But just then they caught sight of the drab, blue denim figure, striding down the street. Even Daisy, the old hound dog, raised her head to look. Saul stood up and ran lickety-split down the road to meet his brother. The others waited. They watched the small denim-clad figure run up to take the metal lunch box from the taller one as he did every night.

Then they saw Caleb's anger. For, he held on to the lunch box when Saul reached for it, and he did not put his hand on the boy's shoulder. Tension mounted with the group on the porch; the day had been hard enough already. They had come to know Caleb's wrath well of late, and it was not pleasant to think of dealing with it tonight. Effie's eyes peered anxiously out on the street for a few seconds and then shifted quickly to her husband's. But she found no comfort there. His attention was still fixed on the tall figure coming up the path and refused to meet her beseeching glance.

Saul traipsed slowly behind his brother, unhappy that his greeting had not been returned more warmly, but at the same time aware that the anger was not intended for him. When he first went up to take the lunch box, he had said in a low tone such as might be used in giving the password to a secret hide-out, "Joe got killed." Caleb's answer had been a brusque "I know," and it was then that he had jerked away. So the younger boy knew it was Joe that made him angry. That made it better because Caleb was his idol and he could not bear to be in disfavor. But at the same time, with all the instinct of his twelve years he knew better than to play with fire.

Caleb did not even say hello as he mounted the front steps. Anger burned red inside him and would not be brushed aside. He felt his mother's eyes on him, but, ignoring her, he turned to his father instead. "Well, Pa," he blurted out, "did y' go by the comp'ny? Did y' see the boss man?"

Asa looked at his son anxiously. He was shocked by the suddenness of the attack; he had not expected Caleb to remember these details quite so quickly. But at the same time he had seen the questions on the boy's face even before they were spoken, and fear had crowded everything else out of his brain. He knew that after the unpleasantness of his afternoon he would never be able to give a satisfactory reply. Fortunately, Effie interrupted. "Sh-h-h, Caleb," she said. "Think o' Ellen."

Caleb was immediately silent; his face jerked around to look at his mother. Now he was really angry—angry with himself as well as the world. Why had he not thought of Ellen? He had feelings as much as the rest of them. He only wanted to help. Even his anger was because of her, because he wanted to see her treated fairly. And instead, he had ended up by hurting her himself.

Ellen, however, was well aware of what was going on, and she wanted to avoid as much trouble as possible. She gathered the sleepy little Dora into her arms and stood up.

"You shouldn' lift 'er, Ellen," Effie scolded. "She too big." Ellen didn't argue, but she didn't put the child down either. She just rubbed her cheek against Dora's woolly head and said, "Come, baby, le's go t' bed." Then she went inside.

Silence followed her departure—a silence in which all eyes were turned to Caleb. His long face was still hard with anger, but it had grown a little sad, a little anxious since his mother's rebuke. "I'm sorry," he said at last. "I guess I wasn't thinkin'." It seemed strange to see his face gray and ashamed and to hear that tone of humility coming from his tall, brawny frame.

But they were not surprised for long. After a brief silence, he took up the question he had asked before. "Well, did y' go by the comp'ny? Did y' talk t' the boss man?"

"Yeah, I talk t' 'im." Asa lowered his eyes to the floor.

"What he say? How much he gonna pay?"

"They gonna pay fo' the fun'ral."

"That all?"

"Yeah, that's all. But I kin—"

"'Notha one o' yo' kind white folks!" Caleb spat vehemently out of the side of his mouth.

"Caleb, I don't 'low nobody t' spit on my flo'," Effie reprimanded. But her soft voice was either ignored or not heard.

For Caleb went on: "That man murdered Joe! . . . Joe, he tell me heself they don' give 'im enough suppo'ts."

"Yeah, I know, I know," Asa soothed. "I'm gonna speak t' Mistah Charles."

"What good that do? He ain't got nothin' t' do wid it. You gotta work it out yo'self."

"He help us. He always do."

"Yeah, good ol' Mistah Charles, he know when he well off. Natcherly, he look out fo' his slaves. Else they might find out they kin do widout him."

"Sh-h-h, Caleb," Effie broke in, her eyes burning with anger. "You know we ain't slaves. . . . 'Tain't right t' talk 'bout Mistah Charles that way. S'pose somep'n happen to 'im? What we do then?"

"We go up no'th an' get rich."

Saul edged closer to his brother. The others—Effie, Henry, Liza—looked anxiously from father to son. This was by no means the first argument begun that way. Those battles were never pleasant, and all of them—except Saul, who enjoyed spurring his brother on to victory—were silently praying that on this night particularly peace might be maintained.

Asa stood up. "Listen, Caleb," he said. "We been through all this. . . . Tonight's hard enough as is. . . . If you wanta argue, go fin' somebody feels the same way. But don' bring no trouble heah."

Caleb looked at his father hard for a moment. The veins swelled in his thick black throat; his full lips formed a narrow pinched line; his face became even more like stone. But, much as he longed to, he did not speak further about the thing eating into him. He just clinched his jaw and turned away. "I got a date anyway," he growled. Then he stamped into the house, through the parlor, up the stairs to his room.

CHAPTER

3

THE strange thing about it was that that night of all nights he did not have a date. Usually he did; scarcely an evening went by that he didn't shave and put on his good pants in preparation for staying out till after midnight. The girls liked him too. Besides being tall and black and broad-shouldered, he had a voice that was strong and deep, a face always animated. Indeed, his whole being was animated. Whenever he spoke about something of importance to him, his voice grew eager, his eyes sparkling black, his body tight and vibrant. He had also an excited way of slamming one fist into the palm of the other hand to emphasize a point.

Tonight, however, all that life had seeped away. By the time he reached his room even the anger had burned out. It was hot and musty in there, and, built up under the eaves as it was, even the weak traces of evening sunlight which haunted the other parts of the house were shut out. But Caleb did not bother to turn on the electric light. He just threw himself onto the broad iron bed and tried, face downward in the pillow, to think of nothing. Since he was dead tired, that was not difficult.

Caleb worked on the railroad from eight o'clock to five o'clock six days a week. He loaded and unloaded freight; he swept up trash; a few times each month he went all the way to Washington and back with the train. But he hated working—how he hated it!—especially the heavy, dirty kind he had to do on the railroad. The only reason he stayed on was because it seemed the closest thing to the traveling he wanted to do.

Caleb was not, however, thinking of that now. He had managed to shut it all out—everything except for the expression on his mother's face when he was arguing with his father. He could never forget that because each time it was the same—calm and gentle but with fear and anger and disbelief burning in the large black eyes. Sometimes those eyes came to torture him even in his sleep. That was why now, when his whole body ached with fatigue, he did not give himself up to it. He could not bear to be awakened by those eyes.

He was conscious then of a tugging at his feet. Because it was annoying, he raised his head enough to peer through the darkness and investigate. Saul was taking off his shoes for him.

"Thanks," he grunted, but the boy did not answer. He finished his job in silence and then sat down on the floor in a corner where he could keep an eye on the bed. He liked doing that; he did it almost every night. It made him feel important and responsible; it made him feel like a soldier on guard while his general slept.

If anything, Caleb was greater than a general to him. Caleb was his idol, a savior, almost a second Christ. He was the one person Saul knew who was not only dissatisfied with things as they were, but also daring enough to say something about them.

"Saul! . . . Saul!" May's shrill voice rang through the thin walls of the house.

"You want suppah?" the boy asked Caleb.

"Na-a-a."

"Ma say fo' you all t' come down right now," May screamed again. "Suppah's gettin' cold."

Saul went to the door and opened it a crack. "We ain't hungry," he bellowed. Then he closed it again and went back to his corner. For a few minutes he sat there, his eyes glued to the long dark form in the bed, wishing that Caleb would stop trying to sleep and talk to him.

Before long his wish came true. Caleb sat up on the edge of the bed. "Think I *will* go out," he said. "Maybe some o' the fellas'll be down t' the sto'."

"Ain't you hungry?"

"Pa tol' me not t' make trouble."

"Couldn' you jest eat an' not say anything?"

"No. . . . I'm too mad. . . . Was the comp'ny's fault Joe got killed. They won't do nothin' 'bout it, neitha. Only jest pay fo' the funeral. Otha places—up no'th, I mean—they wouldn' let 'em get away wid that. But heah—Pa don' even dare take it t' cou't."

Saul listened in awe from his corner, unable, in the darkness, to see his brother, but knowing even so that his teeth were clinched, the muscles in his neck tight and bulging, the black fire burning in his eyes. At twelve, Saul could not really appreciate the reasons for this. He admired it; he admired Caleb's strong, careless, important way of talking. But at the same time he found the whole thing frightening. His mother had taught him from birth not to bother with white children. White and black were two separate things like day and night, like earth and sky, like turnip greens and ice cream. God made it that way, and that was how it was meant to be. Besides, it had always seemed to Saul that God knew best. Therefore, when the one he admired most in the whole world said the exact opposite, he found it difficult to choose between the two.

It might have been easier had he been able to see Caleb's dissatisfaction not only with the world but with himself as well. Even Caleb wondered sometimes how he had grown into the man he was. Now he crossed to the middle of the room to pull the chain for the electric light. Then he stood in front of the small cracked mirror, pulling on his good pants. Every night as he did this, admiring the glow of the electric light on his dark skin, he was amazed by his reflection. He had not always been tall and strong or rebellious and brazen as he was sometimes now. No, he had been raised according to the same principles as Saul.

There had been a time when he did odd jobs for Miss Elizabeth after school and not only respected her but felt a certain pride in doing so. Even now, had he allowed himself, he might have felt the same way. There was safety in living as his father did, peace and comfort in the knowledge that come good times or bad you would always be taken care of. Among the colored people at least, there was also a kind of respect. But Caleb could not allow himself to settle down to that. Though he hated his work at the railroad, dreaded the lifting and hauling so that he could hardly get up in the morning, he felt it necessary to sneer at the alternative.

Most men quite openly preferred jobs as chauffeurs, butlers, gardeners to the hot, grueling work in the railroad yards or laying roads, but Caleb could not have endured wearing a black uniform, unquestioningly obeying orders, saying only "yes sir. . . . yes ma'm" day in and day out. He could not even speak respectfully of his boss man down at the yards as his father did of Mr. Charles. Effie told Asa it was because the people he worked with were like that. But inside, she knew that was not the whole answer. Caleb had always been a crusader; he had never been able to be quiet about injustice. And there was injustice; there always had been. Effie, through her years of wisdom, knew there always would be. But she could not teach that to Caleb; nobody could.

Caleb would not listen to things he did not want to hear. He just got angry like he had tonight and turned away. Saul was the only one he would talk to at such times. For, Saul, though often frightened, was always quite obviously fascinated. He never wanted to make a point; he never asked a difficult question; he never tried to do anything but listen.

Caleb talked to him now as he took his shirt down from the hook on the closet door. "Up no'th," he was saying, "they don' dare treat nobody like they treated Joe. . . . One man's as good as th' otha. . . . You go t' school with white kids up no'th."

"The teacha white?"

"Yeah."

"Don' know's I'd like that."

"Oh, they's colored ones too. . . . An' you kin live wherevah you want, an' go in any place you like, an' sit in the front o' the bus." He tucked the shirt inside his pants.

"You goin' up no'th, Caleb?"

"Maybe. . . . But I don' think so," he mused, struggling with the top button of his shirt. "Think I'll jest maybe try an' make some change heah."

Saul was silent for a few seconds after that. Caleb's last statement had sent a cold stab of fear into the pit of his stomach. He had heard this discussed by others; furthermore, he knew his brother well. It would be nice, of course, to have "one man as good as another"; but Saul was not sure he wanted things any different from the way they were. "You goin' t' see a girl?" he finally dared to ask.

"Yeah, I guess so. . . . Gotta do somethin'."

"Stay home an' play pokah wid me. May's got a date; so do Henry."

"Cain't. . . . I'd kill Pa 'fore the evenin' was up."

In no time at all Caleb had pulled his wallet out of the hole in the mattress and hurried out of the room. He did not even say good-bye.

CHAPTER

4

Joe was killed on the twenty-seventh of April. And, though it was a completely separate event, because of the changes which it entailed, for some time afterwards all the Blakes tended to regard that day as the beginning of their hard luck.

Ellen never went back to the little house she and Joe had rented three blocks away. The day after the funeral Henry and Asa and some of the neighbors loaded the furniture on their cars and wagons and brought it back to the old house on Cameron Street. That would at least save the rent. Besides, Ellen did not want to go back there alone.

That, of course, made conditions more crowded at home. Caleb had long before been moved upstairs to the attic. At first Effie considered putting Henry up there with him, but then she decided against it. Such an arrangement seemed almost to invite trouble. So Saul moved up instead.

Caleb did not like having his privacy intruded upon. But he recognized the necessity for the change and, because he much preferred Saul to Henry, did not complain. Besides, the boy was usually asleep when he came in from his nightly wanderings, and then when he felt like talking, there was always someone who would listen. Also, as time went on, the privacy became a less and less important issue. For, there were many nights when Caleb did not come home at all.

His mother worried about that, of course. She lay awake nights listening for his footsteps. In the morning she asked Saul what time his brother had come to bed. At first Saul, trained to honesty since babyhood, told the truth. But then loyalty to his idol became the master, and he learned to lie with the same innocence he had previously displayed in telling the truth.

Effie, none the wiser, devoted herself to her other worries —the most immediate, of course, being Ellen. Ellen did not languish in her grief or ask for sympathy or humoring because of it. She helped with the mending and the housecleaning. Sometimes when Liza had an extra lot to do, she helped her correct her school papers. At the same time, however, she would not let little Dora out of her sight. She even took her sewing outside to watch the child play. And sometimes when she thought no one was looking she would take the little girl in her arms and sit quietly in a corner kissing the top of the fuzzy head over and over again.

Effie knew she did this, and she did not like it. "Ain't good fo' the chile," she said to Asa more than once. But she did not like to speak to Ellen about it; instead she developed her own way of handling the situation. When the house grew too quiet, when even Dora's piping chatter could no longer be heard, she would call out, "You finish those socks yet, honey?" or "Ellen, come gimme a hand wi' these tomatoes." That always worked.

Still it was too big and busy a household to revolve around one person. May was in a turmoil about a boy named Buddy Linden who began appearing more and more often at the house. She no longer telephoned her father at work; indeed, she rarely even spoke to him at home. She spent most of her evenings—when she was not out—just staring across the porch railing into the empty sky or asking Effie her eternal question: "Listen, Mama—don't you think men like thin girls better 'n fat ones afta all?" But she never stayed for Effie's answer. She was always in too much of a hurry to do something or to get somewhere. Besides, she did not care for lectures on wasting lunch money and burning the candle at both ends.

Henry was the only one Effie didn't have to worry about. He was in love too, but his was an old thing and one of much more comfort to his parents. He was—except for the fact that he could not afford a ring—engaged to Ruby Atwater. She was a nice girl; the Atwaters were a good old family. The match was smiled on by everyone. Every evening they took a walk, winding in and out of the dark, quiet streets and stopping afterwards at either the Atwaters or the Blakes for a cool drink. They never spoke of their love as May did, but people on their porches always smiled knowingly at each other when they saw them pass in the darkness.

Effie worried about Liza too, but the problem she presented was completely different from that of all the others. She was the only one who did not make use of the lengthening days for added hours of pleasure. Whenever the neighbors came to call or met Effie at the grocery store, they asked about Liza. They considered it pretty fine to be a schoolteacher; that was, indeed, one more reason they had for respecting the Blakes. But they never once fell for Effie's feeble apologies about Liza being "too tied up in her school work t' have time out t' play." And they were right; at home the conversation ran quite the other way. "Whyn't y' go out, Liza? Henry ask you a million times t' go with 'im an' Ruby. Ain't right, a girl yo' age sittin' home every evenin'. If you don' watch yo' step, I'm gonna burn that libr'y cahd."

But Liza went right on reading. And Effie never carried out her threat; she could not. For, inasmuch as she, herself, could neither read nor write and Asa had to struggle over both, she stood in great awe of this learned child.

Asa was in some ways more fortunate than his wife.

Whereas he had no pillar of strength to look up to as she had in him, he did not have to stay home with the problems every day either.

Each morning at seven-thirty he called Henry and climbed into the front seat of the Ford. In just the short ten minutes which it took to drive from Cameron Street to the Charles Lawrences' house, he cut himself off from all the difficulties to be dealt with at home. As soon as he got there, he went down cellar and put on the perfectly pressed black outfit which Caleb, in moments of wrath, referred to as his "monkey suit." Then he went upstairs and had a cup of Martha's coffee while waiting for it to be eight-thirty so he could take the breakfast up. Next he cleaned the living room. And after that it was time to drive Mr. Charles to the office, come back and drive Miss 'Liz'beth wherever she wanted to go or do whatever she wanted done. And so it went all day long —drive Mr. Charles here, take Miss 'Liz'beth there; fetch this from the store; serve dinner; wash the car; wax the floors.

But it didn't really go as fast and hard as that. There was plenty of time—especially after dinner—to sit and do nothing if you had a mind to. So always—then and in the long waits he sometimes had in the car—there was plenty of time for Asa's mind to go back to Cameron Street.

He prayed Ellen's baby wouldn't come when he was away. He worried about Liza. He wondered if May would end up marrying her Buddy. And every day—indeed, every hour of every day—he thought about Caleb. It got so that every time he said, "yes, sir" or "yes, ma'm," he could feel the sneering eyes on the back of his neck. When Miss 'Liz'beth let him go home early, he heard the surly, angry voice mock, "Natcherly, Mistah Charles gotta be good t' his slaves."

Those things brought back the quarrels—almost nightly now—and that hurt. For, Caleb, as the oldest boy, had always been the one Asa wanted most to follow in his footsteps. Not be a chauffeur; he would like more for him than that. That was work of the past now, a kind which, in the next generation might not even be considered honorable.

No, that wasn't what Asa meant. He meant a man who went to church every Sunday; who married and raised himself a good healthy family; who made a comfortable home for that family. A man who knew his place in the world and maintained it without overstepping its limits. It looked now as if Caleb were the farthest of any of them from fulfilling that dream. And this above everything else was a bitter, unrelenting disappointment for Asa to accept.

CHAPTER

5

CALEB, himself, never stopped to think what Asa's plans for him might have been. He knew, of course; down in the depths of his soul he knew without even being conscious of it. He never allowed himself to be conscious of things like that.

He did love his parents, too—though he never let himself admit that either. He loved them and, despite himself, he respected them. But at the same time he regarded them—especially his father—with pity. Was it not pitiful to be barely able to read, to be forced to dress up like a trained monkey every day, to have to bow and scrape to another man just to keep your family in food and clothes? And what seemed even more tragic to Caleb was the fact that Asa didn't see his own plight; that he did not seek to remedy it, nor even allow others to. He called it the will of God and said it was the colored man's duty to accept without questioning.

Caleb discussed these things with some of the other men who worked on the railroad. Not with all of them, of course; he was discriminant about whom he talked to. He avoided the white-livered cowards who might blab to the boss man. For, much as he hated it, he could not afford to lose that job.

At first his carefully chosen followers just listened to him like Saul. Later they, too, began to talk. They unquestioningly accepted Caleb as their leader. But the more he said to them, the more he inspired them to think—or even to lead. And before long they were striving ceaselessly to make him aware of their knowledge and zeal.

After several months of arguing and exchanging ideas they finally decided in the middle of May to do something more than talk. There were five of them by then—four besides Caleb—who had become loyal and zealous defenders of the cause. Their names were Jim Rogers, Hiram Jones, Tom Field, and John Greer. They came from the other side of town, the part referred to throughout Millboro as the "rough section." As a child, Caleb, like all the other children in his neighborhood, had been taught to steer clear of people from there. Perhaps that was why he turned to them now.

But also they were more interested in his cause than anybody else. At lunch hour every day the five of them stretched out under one of the big trees near the railroad yards and talked as they ate. They discussed millions of things, of course, because the more they saw of each other the more they had in common. Caleb spent a good part of his nights and evenings in their haunts. They discussed girls, the outrageous cost of a bottle of beer, the previous night's poker hands, and eventually always got back to the mean selfishness of the boss man.

Then Caleb would say, "God damn that man anyhow! . . . Who he think he is? 'Hurry up, hurry up, hurry up. Else this time come off yo' lunch.' Who he think he is anyway?"

"I work fo' a man like that once when I was a kid. . . . He say I loafed. Wouldn' pay me but half."

"What you do?"

"Took de pay an' mo' out of a box in de kitchen cupboard. Took one o' his puppies too; his dog jest have puppies."

"He come aftah you?"

"Na-a-a. They got so much maybe they didn' even know."

"White folks is all like that."

"Yeah. My pa got sent t' jail by a white man."

"How come?"

"I don' know. What's the difference? A white man done it."

"It's different up no'th."

"How you know, Caleb?"

"Oh, ever'body knows that. . . . White folks an' colored folks eat in th' same hotels, sit in same paht o' the bus, go t' the same schools."

"Don' know's I'd like that. Don' know's I'd wanta have that much t' do wid white folks."

"Who would? . . . But at least it's fair—fairer than it is now."

"Yeah. Caleb's right. . . . It's bettah."

"Read in the papah th' otha day wheah some folks wants t' make it the same down heah. You know, get rid o' segergation. They got it in the s'preme cou't now."

"Who want to, Caleb?"

"Oh, the Presi*dent* an' some men in Congress."

"White folks too, eh? . . . Reckon they'll do it?"

But the boss man interrupted there. He bellowed across the yard to them from the shade of another tree. "Hey, you guys, you been layin' there close to an hour an' a half. . . . Back t' work."

They all looked up, but none of them moved. Caleb answered the question put to him before the interruption. "Sure, I reckon they'll do it," he said. "I hope so. . . . There'll be a lot o' kickin', but I ain't afraid t' fight, are you?"

No answer was necessary for that question. These men relished the idea of a fight; it was their entertainment. Anyway there was not time for an answer. The white man called to them again, and, without another word, flicking their cigarette butts on the ground, they obeyed.

CHAPTER

6

THE second week in June Miss 'Liz'beth and Mr. Charles went to New York for a few days. That was nice for Asa. Though Miss 'Liz'beth left a list of things for him and Martha to do, with no dinner to serve they could take off early every evening. It was nice for May too; it meant she got a ride home from work every day.

Always Effie and Liza and Ellen were sitting on the porch waiting for them; it gave Asa a good warm feeling inside to see his family gathered together, happy and secure in their own house. He felt doubly good about it during that week because he drove Martha home, and, while her tiny little house was adequate, the sight of it helped him to realize how much more fortunate he was than his neighbors.

If one was fortunate, he told himself, one must show his gratitude to God by being kind to those who were less fortunate, by working hard and praying hard, by accepting with as few complaints as possible the harsher manifestations of God's will.

His mind was deep in this very thought one evening as he slammed the car door and walked up the path to the house, to the peace and warmth of his family. Effie and Ellen were, as usual, sitting on the front porch. Dora was pulling poor old Daisy by her neck, trying to get her to play but having very little luck. Liza was back in the kitchen finishing up some chores for her mother. As they came up the path, Henry lingered behind to play with Dora, and May rushed ahead, sputtering to her mother about her date for the evening. But Asa walked quietly and undistracted up the front steps. He patted Ellen's shoulder and gave Effie a kiss. Then he sat down and stuffed his pipe with tobacco. "Any news?" he asked at last.

That was Effie's cue. Every evening she gave him a blow-by-blow description of her day. They both enjoyed it. It made Effie feel important and helped Asa to stay a part of things.

"Well, this mo'nin'," she began, "Pearl come ovah."

"Which Pearl?"

"Oh . . . Pearl Higgins. . . . She so happy. —You know I always feel sorry fo' 'er, evah since Sam died, I mean—with that ol' mothah o' hern t' take care of an' that boy t' keep in food an' clothes. . . . But she were so happy t'day. The boy done got a scholarship t' college, same as Liza. . . . Really, Asa you shoulda seen the smile on her face."

"Yeah; I'm glad. How long Sam been dead now?"

"Must be close t' ten yeahs now. The boy was small yet —younger 'n Saul."

"Yeah, Pearl had a hard pull."

"Listen, Mama," May burst in. "Couldn' you press my blue dress fo' me? It's so ha'd, an' I gotta look nice t'night."

But the answer came from her father. "Young lady, if you old enough t' go to a pahty an' stay out half the night, you old enough t' iron yo' own dress."

May skulked out without another word, but Effie spoke up in her defense. "She been wukkin' ha'd all day, Asa. She wohn out."

"So have you. She jest plumb spoiled." Silence. Then he turned to Ellen. "Well, honey, what you do t'day?"

"Nothin' much. It's too hot. Me an' Dora took a walk though. An' you know who we met, Papa? That Elvira

Ross—the one who got into trouble with 'er nephew. An' you know her—ugly as a mud fence an' big as three oil trucks. But she was so sweet wi' that baby. Picked 'er up an' carried 'er when she got tiahed; helped 'er pick a bunch o' clovah an' daisies. An' not the least bit 'shamed, neitha; 's if people hadn' been talkin' 'bout 'er like they has. 'Mo'nin', Elvira,' I says t' her. An' she calls back sweet as anythin', 'Mo'nin', Ellen. How you?' Not the least bit 'shamed. I think it's wondahful she kin ac' like that; I don' think I could."

"That's the only way she could ac'," Effie remarked. "Only—"

But she was cut off at that point by Saul who came running across the yard. "Caleb . . . Caleb," he called. "Caleb home yet?"

"No, he's late again. He always late nowadays."

The boy's face fell with his mother's answer. "Phooey," he said. "I had somethin' t' tell 'im." He sat down disconsolately on the porch steps, head in hands. Daisy came up to lie beside him, her head in his lap, and together they watched the street.

Meanwhile the conversation on the porch continued as before. "You know, Effie, that place May works looks pretty nice. Prob'ly nice people theah."

"Yeah, it's s'pose t' be good. Alma Johnson say Mrs. Pennin'ton goes theah. Bound t' be good if Mrs. Pennin'ton go."

"Wondah how much they pay, women like that, t' get they hair curled."

"Plenty, I reckon. But I don' see the point now they got home permanents. . . . Cou'se, white folks is diff'rent. People like Miss 'Liz'beth an' Mrs. Pennin'ton, they don' have t' worry 'bout money."

Asa smoked his pipe in silence for a few minutes. Then he glanced at the clock on the window sill and noticed that it said five of seven. "Ain't we gonna eat soon?" he asked.

"I wanta wait fo' Caleb. He nevah eat with us any mo'."

Again there was silence.

"Asa . . . I wanta tell you somep'in—somep'in I heard at the sto' t'day. You know, Liza goes with me now school's out. An' this mo'nin', Mistah Jabez, he says t' Liza, 'Well, Miss Liza, see by the papah, you gonna be teachin' white chillun too nex' yeah.' Now, Liza, maybe she already know. Anyhow—you cain't nevah tell with 'er—she says jest as serious an' quiet like, 'Yessuh, Mistah Jabez, that's what they say.' But me—Asa, did you know that?"

"Know what? Sho. I heah talk, but, Effie, don' worry; they been talk like that fo' yeahs."

"No, Asa. It ain't jest talk this time. I didn't undahstand. So, I says t' Jabez, 'What happen, Mistah Jabez?' An' he say, 'Yestiddy evenin' the s'preme cou't make a law 'gainst segergation.' Now, Jabez pretty smaht. You know, Asa, how he sit behin' that countah all day reading the papahs. Cou'se, I don' know the fust thing 'bout s'preme cou't an' segergation. But I don' want nobody like Jabez t' know that. So I says, 'Really? Wha' d' you know?' An' then I ask him 'bout his vegetables. Soon's we got outside though, I ask Liza."

"Yeah, that's right. Liza knows mo' than Jabez; Jabez talk too much."

"But Liza say he right. She say they make a law that white folks an' black folks gotta do things t'gethah. Gotta go t' same school, eat in same places, sit in same paht o' the bus. Liza say it prob'ly won't happen right away though. What you think, Asa?"

"I don' know, Effie, I don' know. Y' nevah can tell what they might do. . . . But I cain't see Saul goin' t' school wid white kids; nor Liza teachin' 'em. I cain't see me sittin' side o' Mistah Charles on the bus neitha. . . . An', Effie, I think they's plenty mo' feel the same way. I hope they don' push 'm."

Ellen was very quiet in her seat in the hammock. She did not understand this kind of talk; nor did she care about it.

Her mind, as usual, was concerned with one thing—the growing, quivering new life within her.

Saul was silent, too. But for a different reason. He listened in awe to the conversation. He leaned back against the porch rail, and in the semi-darkness his black eyes moved solemnly from one face to the other.

"Hey, ain't we gonna eat soon?" It was Henry, come from the yard carrying sleepy Dora. He looked at the clock in the window; it said twenty-five of eight now. Then he looked questioningly at his mother.

Effie glanced at the clock, too. "Well, I guess so," she said sadly. "I thought maybe we'd wait fo' Caleb. He nevah eats with us no mo'." She cast another glance at the clock. "But it *is* late. . . . Henry, you help Ellen put Dora t' bed, an' I'll get suppah on the table."

"Okay."

"I kin do it, Henry."

"No. Lemme help; I like it."

"Awright. But I kin really do it. . . . Dora, come to Mama."

Henry walked towards her, still carrying the child, and Dora held out her arms. But Effie interrupted. "Don' you carry 'er, Ellen; she too big. Tha's why I tol' Henry t' he'p you."

Ellen obeyed without further protest and followed Henry into the house. Asa and Effie went in too, so that only Saul and Daisy remained on the porch.

Saul had to talk to Caleb. Supper or no supper, there was nothing that mattered to him so much as being the first to tell his brother the news.

CHAPTER

7

*I*T was just as well they didn't wait supper for Caleb. Saul grumbled when they made him stop watching and come in to eat. But he obeyed (obedience was a lesson well taught in the Blake household) , and when he got out again at eight-thirty, nothing had happened. He resumed his place on the steps, and Daisy gave up digging holes to come lie down beside him. Otherwise he sat there completely alone.

The others were all busy. May's Buddy had come before they were even finished eating. And no sooner had Saul settled down to his watch again than Henry went off to see Ruby. Asa and Ellen came out then, but they did not sit down. They were going to take a walk while Liza and Effie finished cleaning up in the kitchen. Asa asked Saul to go along with them, but the boy's subdued answer made it clear he would rather stay there.

Asa understood the reason, and puckers formed in the high forehead of his long serious face. But he did not speak. He had promised to see that Ellen got some exercise before she went to bed. That was his immediate duty, and anything he could have said would only have thwarted his purpose. He simply took Ellen's arm in his and led her gently down the path to the sidewalk.

At nine o'clock Liza and Effie came out. They were talking and did not bother to lower their voices. Saul listened curiously; he knew it was Caleb they were discussing.

43

"He nevah been latah than this," Effie said. "I'm beginnin' t' think maybe somep'in happen to 'im."

"Oh, don' worry, Mama. Mos' likely he jes' went home wi' somebody fo' suppah."

"He won't dressed propah to."

"Oh, Mama, that don't mattah. He work wi' those men all day. They jes' as messy as he is."

"Well, I hope you right. He's awful late. . . . Worries me, too, 'cause of what Jabez said t'day. But I don' reckon he know yet."

Saul thought his mother was right. But he didn't say anything; he just stared out into the darkness.

When the other two came back from their walk, Ellen said she was going to bed, and Effie told Saul it was time he went too. But the boy did not move, and his mother said nothing further until the hands of the clock pointed to quarter past ten. Then she said, "Saul, I tol' you a good while back t' go t' bed. Now go."

"I jes' wanta stay up till Caleb comes home."

"Ain't no tellin' when Caleb comin'. An' when he do, he'll wake you up. He'll have to—gettin' int' bed. . . . Now, go on upstaihs."

Saul didn't move.

"You heah yo' ma, Saul?"

"Yessuh."

"Then mind. . . . You ain't too big fo' my belt."

Very quietly the boy stood up and went into the house, leaving the other three to sit there, their anxious minds communing in the dead silence, for nearly an hour more. Then Henry came home.

"Well," Asa said, "I reckon we all bettah go t' bed."

"You all go 'long," Effie replied. "Somehow I jest ain't tihad yet."

After some hesitation both Henry and Liza went inside.

"Come, Effie," Asa said. "You know May don' evah come in till late."

"I know. I ain't worried 'bout May."

"No sense worryin' 'bout Caleb, neitha. We got work t' do in the mo'nin'. Ain't no tellin' when he'll come home. Ain't nothin' you can do by settin' up an' frettin' neitha."

"You reckon he in trouble, Asa?"

"Mos' likely he jes' havin' a good time."

"Y' know, Asa, sometimes—even when he talk mean like he do—I think I love 'im mo' than any of 'em. He ain't a bad boy, Asa."

"No, he ain't. He jes' headstrong; don' know how things really is yet. But he'll learn, I reckon. I hope he will."

"You don' think he's in trouble?"

"No. Come on t' bed now. You'll be wo' out t'morrah."

When Saul heard the boards squeek over by the door, he opened his eyes and looked out at the sky as he had done a million times that night. But this time the sky was gray and when he turned over he saw a dark figure standing over the bed. "That you, Caleb?" he asked, sitting up with a start.

"Sh-h-h . . . Yeah it's me. Was Pa mad?"

"Wheah you been?"

"Sh-h-h. Wait'll I close the do'."

"You heah 'bout the s'preme cou't? 'Bout no segergation?"

"Yeah, that's wheah I been."

"Wheah?"

"We had a meetin'."

"A meetin'?"

"Yeah. They's plenty, y' know, been waitin' fo' this fo' a good while. We ain't gonna let nobody stop it. Nobody like Mama an' Pa always talkin' 'bout 'respect' an' 'good Mistah Charles' an' 'sweet Miss 'Liz'beth.' "

"You mean you got a gang? What you gonna do?"

"Nothin'—yet. We gotta wait. Maybe we won't nevah do nothin'!"

"Oh." There was a trace of disappointment in Saul's voice. A long silence followed because he did not know what else to say. There were a lot of questions which sprang to his mind, but he did not dare. Finally he just said, "It's mo'nin' already; you still want me t' wake you up the reg'lar time?"

"Naw, don' wake me up."

"But yo' boss'll be mad if you late."

"No. I quit." Caleb climbed into bed beside Saul and turned his face to the wall. By that time Saul no longer feared his brother's anger. A new fear—a concern for the safety of his idol—had replaced any he might have had for himself. He reached his hand across the pillow and touched Caleb's cool, hard shoulder. "Listen, Caleb," he asked urgently, "You ain't in trouble, is you? . . . You didn' do nothin' t'night, did ya?"

Caleb did not turn over. But it made him feel good inside to know that somebody—even this little boy—really cared about him. He knew he should be angry with the boy for even insinuating that he must be careful to stay out of trouble. But then there was moisture in his eyes, and he could not be angry. Instead, he put his large, coarse hand up to cover the small one on the pillow. "No, Saul," he whispered, "I ain't in trouble."

At breakfast the next morning Saul told them Caleb had come home, that he was upstairs asleep and was not going to work. He did not tell them all the details—about the gang, about the meeting, why he was not going to work. He was afraid that might start trouble, trouble which Caleb at the moment would not be able to cope with.

Even so, he saw his mother's large eyes turn in fright towards his father whose lips grew thin and straight. "Well, work o' no work," Asa said, "I'm goin' right up an' talk to 'im."

"Oh, Asa, he mus' be tihad."

"Yeah. I'm tihad too." Effie refilled his coffee cup, and he took another hot biscuit from the plate in the middle of the table. " 'Wake o' not, no son o' mine 's gonna stay out all night 'thout an explanation."

Saul slipped down from the stool he was sitting on and headed stealthily for the stairs. Effie's eyes followed him; still she said nothing. Liza and Henry continued eating in silence. But Asa was not blind. "Saul," he said loudly, a suspicion of anger in his imperative tone, "come back heah an' finish yo' breakfas'."

The boy returned slowly—hesitantly—looking uncertain as to whether to obey or not. When he reached his seat again, he stood beside it for a moment without sitting down. Asa looked up from his plate, and then the anger which his tone had only hinted at before flashed from his eyes.

"Listen, boy," he said loudly and with exaggerated clearness, "you jes' look aftah yo'self. Min' yo' own business, an' don' go tryin' t' save somebody else. They's gonna be trouble 'round heah maybe, but I don' wanta heah no talk 'bout you bein' in it." He glared silently at Saul, who, apparently cowed, resumed his place in front of a plate of eggs.

All eyes turned secretly, under lowered lids, to watch Asa. He stood up, drained the last drop from his coffee cup, and left the room. A terrible stillness followed his departure, a stillness in which Effie's continuous movements at the sink seemed unusually loud. Warily Saul slipped down from his stool again and headed for the door. There he hesitated for a moment, half expecting the others to call him back.

But they did not. Even Liza, who at times like this often had more control of the situation than her mother, only looked after him with accusing eyes. Soon he was upstairs, lurking restlessly outside the closed door. He failed in his first attempt to look through the keyhole, but decided immediately afterwards that it was of little consequence. For the voices inside came to him clearly.

First there was Asa: "Caleb . . . Caleb . . . Caleb, sit up. I wanta talk t' you."

Then there was a heavy heaving of the covers and a low groaning sound.

"Caleb . . . Caleb, I mean it. I ain't got all day t' stand heah. Get up."

"God damn it! Go 'way!"

"Caleb!"

The bedclothes heaved again, and Saul knew by the loud thud which followed that Caleb must be standing in the middle of the floor glaring at his father.

"What you mean carryin' on this way? Wheah you been?"

"Ain't none o' yo' business."

"Sho it is. You my son; this my house. Whatevah happens is my business."

"Listen, Pa. I'm twenty-two. I kin run my own life. I don' need you t' tell me what t' do; an' I don' have t' listen neitha."

"Wheah was you las' night?"

No answer.

"Wheah was you las' night?"

"Okay, I'll tell you wheah I was. . . . They got a new law, Pa—a law says no mo' segergation. . . . I aims t' see that law works. Tha's wheah I was. Out helpin' the law. . . . Whatcha got t' say 'bout that?"

Momentary silence. Then— "Jes' min' you stay outa trouble. These is white folks' laws; white folks, they don' want colahed folks playin' wid deir laws. . . . This heah's a good fam'ly. We got a name—a name been good fo' yeahs an' yeahs. An' don't you hurt it, Caleb. Don't you hurt nobody in dis house."

There was no answer, but Saul, who by now had his eyes

in the crack of the door, saw Caleb's face go hard and bitter, saw his eyes, cruel and arrogant, bore mercilessly into his father's soul.

"Now git up," Asa continued in a somewhat softer tone. "Git up. Put on yo' clothes an' go t' work. . . . You cain't take off f'om work jes' 'cause you decide t' stay up all night. . . . Hurry up. You late already. Wanta git fihad? . . . Put on yo' clothes an' I'll give you a ride."

"Shut up an' stop tellin' me what t' do! I ain't goin' t' work 'cause I quit yestiddy, 'cause I got mo' impo'tant things t' do." Then, as a final blow, he bellowed, "Get the hell out o' heah an' lemme sleep!"

Saul moved aside just in time to give his father right of way out of the room. Asa came out so quickly that he did not even see Saul. His tread was heavy, his lips pressed tight, his strong face gripped by sadness and anger. He walked slowly back down the stairs, and Saul, after his departure, crept back to the open doorway.

Caleb was no longer standing in the middle of the room. He had thrown himself onto the bed again, his face thrust downward in the mattress, his strong hands gripping the bars of the bed. Great heaving sobs shook his whole muscular frame.

Saul saw this and was certain now that something dangerous was afoot. He wanted very much to put his hand gently on the back of that tight-tendoned neck, perhaps to have the whole frightening story poured out to him. But this was Caleb; this was his powerful, unyielding hero. Saul had never seen him cry before. And so, finding himself incapable of anything else, he shut the door and went outside.

CHAPTER

8

*I*T was noon before Caleb came out of the room. Not long after Saul had shut the door and left him, the mighty sobs smothered themselves out in the mattress and gave way to a sleep of utter exhaustion. That sleep was short-lived, however. Suddenly he heard a voice crying, "He's dead! He's dead!" And when he looked down, his father was at his feet, face down on the floor. And he—Caleb—was holding a bloody knife!

He woke from that in a cold sweat and then was afraid to sleep again. Instead he spent the whole morning in inescapable self-torture. First, thinking of the things his father had said, anger flamed inside him. Then he remembered what he had said, and an aching remorse twisted his throat, brought fresh tears to his eyes.

At last, realizing how futile it was to lie there, longing for a sleep which he could not allow himself to indulge in, he got up and dressed. The dead silence of the house made him uneasy, and its semi-darkness with all the shades pulled down against the noonday heat eerily reminded him of the atmosphere in his dream. It was better once he got downstairs where he could hear Ellen's gentle voice prattling to Dora. But still he wanted to avoid them. So, instead of going to the porch, he turned into the kitchen.

In another moment he was sorry. For, Effie was there—

standing at the sink washing greens. "Mo'nin', Caleb," she said. "You hungry?" She was careful to keep her too-revealing eyes concentrated on the sink.

"No, Mama. Thanks," he answered, "I'm goin' out. I'll get somethin' later."

"What time you comin' back?"

"I don' know."

"You be heah fo' suppah?"

"I don' know."

"Don' make yo' pa mad again," she pleaded.

"Oh, hell wid him! I'll do what I damn please!" He walked rapidly from the kitchen, straight through the hall and out the front door. Saul was sitting on the steps. He looked up but did not speak.

"Hello, Saul." Caleb stopped to watch the younger boy pat Daisy. He wished he would ask a question or tell him a piece of news. But Saul was silent. He was still afraid and, after his first look upwards, kept his eyes on the dog.

Caleb could not stand it. "C'mon, walk down the bus stop with me," he said.

"Okay." Saul stood up. He was happy again, still afraid of what Caleb might be plotting in his mind, but glad at least that he was not to be excluded from it. "Caleb, wheah was you las' night? . . . Really to a meetin'?"

Caleb looked at him sideways for a second before replying. "First we had some beer. Then we sat an' talked 'bout how things is gonna be. . . . An' yeah—they was a meetin' too. We 'lected officahs; I'm pres'dent." He said this last proudly, glancing at Saul to catch his response.

He was not disappointed either. The boy looked up at him and grinned, his eyes shining with pride. "Gosh!" he gasped. "Gosh! . . . Could you take me to a meetin' some day, Caleb?"

"Some day, sho. Only not now; we gotta be specially careful now. It's too early t' take a chance on bein' caught."

They had reached the bus stop and, looking up the street, saw the bus in the distance. "Wheah you goin', Caleb?"

"Got some work t' do."

"To a meetin'?"

"No . . . Somethin' else."

"Oh . . . 'Bye."

" 'Bye." The tall black figure swung up the steps of the bus, and the doors eased to behind him.

From then on Caleb was almost never at home. That first night of anxiety and anger and sadness was followed by many others equally as bad. The only difference was that no one dared speak of it any more. They hinted about it among themselves, said little subtle things to comfort each other. But no one ever made a direct statement about it. Asa would catch Effie's worried eyes watching the clock long after the supper dishes had been put away, and he would say, "Don' fret, Effie. Won' do no good." Or in the night when Asa kept climbing out of bed to listen for footsteps on the stairs, Effie would murmur, "He's grown, Asa; he kin take care o' hisself. An' even if he cain't, y' gotta let 'im try."

Sometimes at supper May in her careless, jabbering way would remark, "Well, Caleb sho is gettin' highfalutin. Don' even eat wid us no mo'." But there was always dead silence after something like that—dead silence bristling with tension. Perhaps May didn't feel it—she was too much buried in herself and in her Buddy—but all the others certainly did. Asa, realizing the futility of them, had put a stop to the bellowing scenes between Caleb and himself. But there were times when he would have been glad to have even those rather than the long silences or, worse still, the carefully guarded conversations.

The tension remained—the sadness and the anger, too, mellowing only slightly with time. But eventually the very time which could not comfort them taught a lesson. Whereas they could not forget Caleb's behavior, could not even accept it, it came to the point that they expected it. Effie began putting supper on the table every evening at seven o'clock sharp without even setting a place for Caleb. Asa went to sleep at night instead of staying awake to listen for footsteps on the stairs. Saul rolled over automatically in the gray hours of the morning to make room for the great lanky figure to fall into bed beside him. He tiptoed out of the room at seven o'clock and did not come back until eleven-thirty when he tried to get his brother to tell him some of his escapades.

And Caleb did tell him a little; he could not stop himself. It made him feel important and besides, he told himself, it was good to have as many people as possible—especially young people—interested in the cause.

He really didn't talk much though. He was still very cautious and knew that even sharing his secrets with faithful Saul was taking an unnecessary risk. He told him only the barest essentials—about the meetings, about how many came —men and women, what they expected to gain through the new law. But never the names of the people who came, never the place where they held the meetings, never the means they would use to get their due from the law. Besides, he was never there long enough for much talk. Saul came up at eleven-thirty, and by twelve o'clock Caleb was on the bus for town.

CHAPTER

9

C_{ALEB} was spending almost all his time across town in the "rough section." He had—it is true—aroused a good number of supporters in that neighborhood, but he really went there because that was where all his old friends from the railroad yards lived. They had quit the same day as he, and now they, too, devoted most of their time to the cause.

They were not, however, the ardent believers Caleb was. They felt no strong sense of injustice, or sought to right any great wrong. They followed Caleb solely for the thrills they hoped to get and for the approval of their neighborhood. And they were heartily approved of. Though Caleb's family did not, all the other boys' families knew what they were about and were very proud. The five of them met at one house one day and at another the next to talk and plot and plan. Their mothers fed them well and were especially pleased to have Caleb because they knew he was the leader.

There were very few like Hiram Jones' mother, who closed her doors to them. A hard-working widow who took in washing, she declared that white folks had always been plenty kind to her and that anybody fool enough to get entangled in such matters deserved whatever punishment came his way. She also called them a bunch of loafers who should think of a safer excuse for laying off work. Hiram Jones' was the one place they could not go.

There was a store called Roe's where they went more often than anywhere else. It sold all kinds of things—candy, cigars, aspirin, hot-water bottles, bread, magazines, ice cream. But they went there for the beer. Roe liked them. He was a big, flabby, black man in his fifties, but he was their most loyal supporter. For every bottle of beer they bought (using the money which they managed to work out of their families) he gave them one free. Sometimes they sat around a table in a corner, but more often they lounged in the empty room behind the shop.

The discussion usually revolved around Caleb. But they did not always agree with him, and often, more eager for thrills than results, they became impatient.

"Y' cain't jes' dive in," Caleb said to them more than once. "Y' gotta give 'em a chance t' follow the law."

"Yeah, but how much chance you gotta give 'em? How long you gonna wait?"

"Yeah, we cain't jes' sit 'round an' talk the rest o' our life. Time we did somethin'. How long you mean t' wait, Caleb?"

"Till fall, till the schools open. Then we see what they really aim t' do."

"Whyn't we staht now? The longah you wait, the hahdah it'll be."

"We could jes' ride on buses—sittin' in the front, or go t' the *ho*tel, or go t' the movies an' sit wheah the white people sits," Tom Field spoke up. He always had a plan for quiet rebellion. "What kin they do t' us anyway?" he always said, "Only kick us out. An' that'd git in the papahs. That'd help; anything in the papahs 'd help. . . . 'Sides, we got the law."

But Caleb even had an answer for that: "Not yet we ain't. I don' undahstand it well's I should, but I think they's a certain 'mount o' time 'fore it has t' be in effect."

Jim Rogers was the only one who stayed out of these discussions. He mostly just leaned against the wall and listened with his brow in a dark scowl. And when he did speak, it was always the same— "We waited too long awready."

As a matter of fact, Roe was the only one in complete agreement with Caleb's conservative ideas. But as he was liked and respected by them all, that was the best support Caleb could have had. He really needed it too. For, despite the angry words he had spluttered at home, despite the easy, positive way he had of talking to his cohorts, Caleb was afraid—terribly, terribly afraid. Sometimes he looked around him at the crowd of people at the meetings (they were held in the vacant lot behind an old church) at the dilapidated condition of Roe's store, at the hard, ravenous faces of the other young men, and he wondered with awe and terror how he had ever managed to get himself into this situation.

He stood there in the darkness and could see the lighted candle shake with his quivering hand. Sometimes there were nearly a hundred people, and though he could not see them, he could hear their breathing as they tried to silence it. "Perhaps some of them are afraid too," he would think, and that was a help. Also, when he remembered how much these people depended on him he could not let them down. Though his hand continued to shake, his voice came out strong and clear. "We got a right to all these things. We always had a right. But now they's a law. Now they gotta live up t' what they always say. . . . We gotta give 'em a chance t' do it, though. If they don't, we'll make 'em, but we gotta give 'em time. . . . We don' wanta hurt nobody; we don' wanta kill our chances 'fore they come true. We gotta be careful; we gotta be patient an' wait."

The people never clapped at the end of his speeches; they had been warned not to. Instead, when he blew out his candle, they just melted like mist into the darkness without so much as a whisper. Then Caleb would go over to Roe's to drown his fear in beer—or something stronger if Roe would provide it.

But some of Caleb's fears could not be drowned by anything. For instance—though he never really thought Jake Greer meant it, prickles of perspiration sprang to his forehead when he heard him say, "Jes' take guns an' make people do what the law say." At times like that or in the early hours of the morning when he was walking alone through the dark streets to catch his bus, he even considered giving the whole thing up and going back to the security of his job in the railroad yards. He never allowed himself to think about that for long, however. His determination and hatred of injustice were too strong. Besides, he knew that he was too far in to get out now. So he went ahead with his campaign. But the fear never left him.

CHAPTER

10

THE rest of the family—even Saul—had almost no knowledge of what was going on in Caleb's world. This, of course, was largely because he was so tight-lipped. But besides that, for a while they were too busy to even wonder about it. They were facing various little crises every day.

Saul took a job on a Pepsi-Cola truck. One day the driver got drunk in a town over forty miles away. The police carted him off to jail and put the boy on a bus for home. So there was a happy ending after all. But in the meantime, the whole of Cameron Street was beside itself with worry.

And May never seemed to have a calm moment. Every night at supper, she talked about how wonderful Buddy was, about what he had said to her the night before, about his latest present. They were not yet engaged, but, as she said at least once a day, it was only because Buddy insisted on getting her a ring even though he could not afford it.

The biggest event of all, however, was the birth of Ellen's baby. It arrived a little after midnight, in the early morning of July sixth—a squirming, gurgling, five-pound baby girl. Ellen was upset at first because it was not a boy she could name Joe. She sobbed out the tears which had been stored inside her for weeks. But when Liza suggested that she might still name the child Joanna, calling her Jo for short, she cheered up again and began to show a real interest in looking after the little thing. After three days she was back at home.

Then what a turmoil of happy excitement engulfed the house. Of course, Caleb was never at home and Henry and Asa and May worked all day. But, surprisingly enough, May loved to talk and giggle to the little thing when she came home in the evening. Asa declared it was just like old times with a baby in the house again. Effie and Liza almost came to blows trying to take care of it. And even Saul, if he thought no one was watching, would stand and stare at the little creature in the old crib. Indeed, it was not until Ellen determinedly demanded full possession of both her children that they remembered the new addition was hers.

Yes, the house was busier than ever—so busy in fact that Asa had to do something he never did; he had to let home interfere with his work. Shortly after the birth of the baby, Mister Charles and Miss Elizabeth planned a two-week vacation at the seashore. They wanted both Martha and Asa to go with them. But when the time came, despite all Effie's persuasion, Asa did not feel he could leave. And in the end he got his brother's boy, Herman, to go instead.

Asa was glad afterwards that it had worked out that way. He had half of each day to spend at home. And besides, only four days after the departure a new calamity befell the family. Saul knew about it first; he heard it from two men drinking beer at Mr. Jabez's store. At first he could hardly believe it. Then he felt hurt that Caleb hadn't told him himself. But he was too loyal to carry the story home; so instead, he just locked it inside his fearful heart.

It was, however, not long before both Effie and Asa knew too. Henry told them; he had heard it from Jerry Moss one evening at a barn dance. Jerry's girl came from across town, and they were dancing in the set next to the one Henry and Ruby were in. The two couples exchanged no conversation, but at one point Henry thought he saw Jerry point at him. And at the next rest period Jerry came over to them.

"See yo' brotha's tryin' a diff'rent kind o' girl these days!" He laughed in a not-too-gentle tone.

At first Henry thought he was talking about Saul. He had not heard the boy was interested in girls yet. But then Saul was quiet about everything. Besides, people were often amused by him. So Henry grinned too. "Wha' d' you mean?"

"Yeah. Saw 'im the otha night."

"Wheah?"

" 'Cross town. Pretty good-lookin' gal too."

When Jerry said that, Henry realized it could not be Saul he was talking about. There was only one member of the Blake family who would even have ventured across town, and even this vague reminder of his older brother made every little hair on Henry's body stand on end. He struggled to appear unruffled, however, and with feigned amusement he mumbled, "Oh, yeah?"

"Yeah. Pretty good lookin' if you go fo' white gals. . . . Me, they make my skin crawl."

The artificial grin dropped from Henry's face. His eyes grew large, and even if he had been able to think of something to say, he could not have gotten the words out.

"Yo' whole fam'ly gonna be like that now?" Jerry continued with a sneer. "You all want white gals now?"

But Henry was silent, and finally, disappointed by so little response, Jerry went away. Ruby turned a frightened face up to Henry. "He talkin' 'bout Caleb?" she asked.

"Yeah."

"You reckon it's true?"

"I don' know. Prob'ly, the way he's been actin'."

Ruby said nothing more, only stood there for a few minutes looking up at him. After two more dances they went home.

Though it was only eleven-thirty when Henry got home, Effie and Asa had already gone to bed. They had become hardened, through Caleb's behavior, to the fact that their children could get themselves home at night. Ordinarily,

Henry tiptoed up to bed, careful not to disturb anyone. But this night was different; this night he bore news which could not be kept.

He stole silently into his parents' bedroom, and, standing by the head of the bed, whispered, "Papa . . . Papa."

Effie was the first to wake. She bolted upright and spluttered in a soft but excited voice, "Wha'sa mattah, son? Wha'sa mattah?"

The jerk of her body woke Asa. He twisted around, groaning in his sleep. Then his eyes opened wide, and he stared in surprise up at Henry's face. "What is it?" he asked in a voice restrained and still cloudy with sleep. "What is it, son?"

"Papa, I gotta talk t' you."

Asa asked no questions. He swung his legs over the side of the bed, rubbed the sleep vigorously from his eyes, and stood up.

Effie remained in her sitting position, watching the two of them. "Turn on the light, Henry," she said.

"Naw, Mama. Tha's okay. We'll go downstairs." And Effie did not answer or argue with that. She knew better than to interfere when her men had something to discuss alone. She just sat there in silence and watched after them as they went out the door.

Asa led the way. In the kitchen he flicked on the light and in the same motion turned to face Henry. "What is it?"

"Caleb."

Asa's face grew even more hollow than usual, his eyes even larger. "Caleb?" He swallowed hard. "What about Caleb?"

Henry pointed to one of the wooden chairs. Asa sat down, and the younger man, still standing, commenced his story. "I seen Jerry Moss t' the dance t'night. He come ovah t' me an' he say, 'Yo' brotha goin' wid a new kind o' gal, ain't he?'

"Me, I don' know what he's talkin' 'bout. I think mebbe Saul; so I says, 'Huh?'

"An' he says, 'Seen Caleb the otha night wid a good-lookin'

gal—if you like that kind.' I didn' say nothin'. So he says, 'Yeah, I seen 'im wid a white gal.' . . . I couldn' b'lieve it; I 'mos fell ovah. Then he says, 'All you fam'ly like that? You all want white gals now?' "

By this time Henry was completely out of breath. But he realized with one glance that his father was even more overcome than he had been. Asa sat doubled over in the chair, his elbows propped on his knees, his face buried despairingly in his long black fingers.

He sat there for a long time like that with Henry, who did not stir, staring down at him. Then, suddenly he jerked himself into an erect position. "Damn that boy!" he burst out furiously. "This time I'm gonna teach 'im a lesson he won' nevah fo'git—nevah, nevah, nevah—long as he live!" He slapped his hand against his knee and stood up. But even this outburst had not satisfied him to the point of returning to bed. On the contrary, his decision for action had set him burning with restlessness. He began to pace the room like a caged animal.

"Evah since he was a chile," he continued, "we teach him right f'om wrong. We teach 'im t' have respect, t' pray, t' be what the Lawd meant 'im t' be. We teach 'im jes' like we teach you an' Saul. And now what happens? He go an' do the 'zact opposite t' what we teach."

Henry said nothing; there was nothing to be said. He just sat down in one of the hard wooden chairs and listened to his father's endless lament. Asa continued to pace the room. "A white woman!" He shook his head. "You cain't go much fahthah, Henry. . . . All his life he been tol' 'white's white an' black's black.' An' now wid his big ideas 'bout equality, he done laid down the most impohtant laws he evah learnt."

Once again Asa collapsed onto one of the hard little chairs. He hung over with his elbows braced against his knees and his head between his legs. "An' now it ain't jest his own life he's wreckin'," he continued. "Now it's the whole fam'ly's.

. . . Blake's a good name, Henry. White folks an' black know that, an' they respect it. But they won't aftah this. . . . What 'ould you think of a fam'ly turned out a boy like that?"

Henry made no reply. After a long silence Asa stood up. "I'm gonna go talk t' yo' ma," he said. "Think it's bettah I tell 'er than she heah t'morrow at de sto'."

CHAPTER

11

THEY waited up the rest of the night for Caleb to come home. When Asa sat on the edge of the bed and retold the story as gently as possible, Effie did not give way at all. But the expression on her face—or rather the lack of expression—made Asa feel more tired and desperate than ever. Her large black eyes swelled wide and deep. Still, not a single tear escaped her eyelids.

She just sat there in bed, staring incredulously at her husband. "I think," she said at last, "I think you oughta talk to 'im. Maybe if you stay up t'night an' talk while he's too tihad t' argue. Then maybe he'll listen. If he only listen, Asa, I know he'll see what's right. If only he listens."

That was only one o'clock; they had a long wait after that. They went down to the kitchen where Effie made ham sandwiches and a pot of coffee. And they sat there slumped over the table until nearly five o'clock. Everyone else was asleep, and the old house—except for an occasional mournful creak—was silent. Even the two of them at the table did not speak, and when by mistake their eyes encountered one another, they looked down again quickly. Each found his own pain sufficient.

Finally, just as they had given up hope of seeing Caleb that night at all, the front door opened and shut; heavy, though guarded, footsteps creaked through the hall to the kitchen. Asa had stood up at the sound of the latch, and he and Caleb met head on in the kitchen doorway.

As if by reflex, Caleb sprang back at sight of his father. But he was, as Effie had anticipated, very tired. And, what is more, he was frightened. He had spent the whole day at Roe's store, and now he realized as never before how fast the impatience was growing among his supporters, how little longer they would allow him to wait.

Then, in the evening he had gone out again with Trudy Reese. How he hated doing that! There was nothing in the whole business he dreaded so much. In the first place, despite her red fingernails and the thick make-up she put on her face to cover the pimples, she was not pretty. Her blond hair was coarse and stiff like a horse's, and her flesh, white as it was, hung on her so loose and sickly-looking that it seemed dirty. But more important than that, she was not a nice girl; anybody could see that. Every time she looked at him he felt as if she were asking him to come to bed—and asking him not because he was himself and she loved him but simply because he was a man. Besides, who could have respect for a white girl willing to go out with a colored man? Still he had had to do it tonight, and he would have to do it again. It was necessary to keep Tom and Jake pacified— and for himself, too. He had to show the world—the stupid, blind world—that he meant what he said when he preached equality.

Nevertheless, it sickened him. Often he thought of home, of the principles drilled into him since infancy, and longed with all his heart to be weak and return to that cast-off security. That was why he stiffened so instantly at sight of his father. It was either that or a violent flood of tears.

Asa spoke to him gently, extending his hand to touch the boy's shoulder. "Come in an' eat, son," he said. "We ain't had a chance t' talk in a long time."

Caleb looked hesitantly at each of them in turn. He saw

the stricken expression on his mother's face, but, though he knew it was a danger signal, still could not resist. Slowly, uncertainly, watching them suspiciously, he came in and sat down at the table. Effie went to the refrigerator and came back with a sandwich and a bottle of Coca-Cola which she set down before him. She hesitated for a moment beside his chair, longing to kiss the rough, short-cropped head. But at the same time, knowing better, she took her seat on the other side of the table.

They let Caleb eat first; they did not ask questions or comment on his lateness. Effie talked about the new baby, and Asa told them about old Lula Press who went down town to collect her pension every Saturday but never told her eight children about it because she wanted help from them too. Caleb was silent, but still the conversation went on. It was almost as if he had been away for a long time and they were bringing him up to date with the news.

Caleb was not fooled, however. He knew something was coming, and when Effie stood up and said she was going back to bed, the boy's tired, drawn face grew even more tense and suspicious. When she had gone, he was very careful to keep his eyes focused on the empty plate before him.

Asa waited no longer. "I wanta talk t' you, son," he said.

"I know that." The arrogant tone had already returned.

"Wheah you been lately? What you been doin'?"

"Tha's my bus'ness."

"Mine too. I'm yo' pa."

"I don' care who you are."

"Yo' ma worries, Caleb. We only wants t' help."

"Oh, shut up!"

"We got a right t' know what you doin' an' wheah you at."

"Eh-h-h-h! T' hell wid it!" Caleb pushed back his chair and brought his hand down with a crack against the table top. "God damn it! Listen," he said, "I kin run my own life. I been workin' fo' fo' yeahs, an' I don' need nobody t' say, 'What you doin'? Wheah you goin'? Who you goin' wid? What time you comin' back?' I don' need dat an' I ain't gonna stan' fo' it eitha! See? I ain't gonna take it!" His voice grew louder and louder; by the time he reached the last words, he was bellowing.

At this point Asa's temper began to give way too. They were both standing, glowering at each other across the kitchen table. Asa retorted, his voice louder and tinged with impatience, "If you acted like you could take care o' yo'self, nobody'd ask you those questions."

"Oh, shut up! You know I look out fo' myself!"

"Listen, Caleb, listen. . . . They's a limit. Bad 'nough t' see you wreckin' yo' own life; breaks yo' ma's heart. But y' gotta draw a line when y' staht ruinin' the chances of yo' whole fam'ly."

"Oh, hell! I heard that evah since I was a kid— 'We a good fam'ly. Folks respects us. We gotta live up t' our reputation.' I say 'shit!' on that reputation!"

"I ain't gonna argue o' try t' tell you wha's right. I know it ain't no use; you been taught that already. . . . But I don' nevah wanta heah no talk o' white gals again. Nevah again! Tha's the worst y' can do!" Asa's voice was loud, but still he managed to keep himself from yielding completely to his anger.

Caleb, however, tense and exhausted from the start, was now beyond all reasoning. The veins in his neck swelled out thick and tight; his eyes had become wild and vacant, his jaw set like iron. "I'll go out wid any damn gal I want!" he burst forth anew. "Black o' white o' red o' blue, what diff rence do the colah make? White gal's as good as any colahed gal. . . . Ain't none o' yo' business who I take out! An'—" He leaned menacingly across the table towards his father; the next few words came slow and soft. "I don' nevah wanta be tol' that agin." He slammed his hand against the table; then he stamped across the room to the doorway while Asa just stood there beside the table, staring after him in heartbroken amazement. In the hallway Caleb turned again, as a cruel boy might to sling one last stone at a dying bird. "The whole damn lot o' you can go straight t' hell!" he screeched. Then, with all the noise of a runaway freight car, he bounded wildly up the rickety old staircase.

Saul had been sitting at the top of the stairs ever since he was first wakened by the loud voices below. He barely had time to get back to bed before Caleb came hurtling into the room. Saul shut his eyes and lay very still. Then the bed lurched under new weight, and he could feel Caleb's body warm against him.

The boy lay there in silence for a long time, very still, afraid to even open his eyes. Caleb did not stir either, and when Saul dared to look, he saw that he was in the same position as when he fell into the bed. His head was face down in the pillow, his feet hanging over the foot of the bed, his hands clenched at his sides. And then Saul realized something else. The tiny jerking of the mattress which he had thought was caused by his brother's heavy breathing or perhaps even by scratching came from neither. Looking carefully at the figure beside him, he saw that, though there was no noise, it was shaken by inexorable sobs.

Because long beams of sunlight were beginning to work their way across the room, Saul could see all this easily. But he did not stay to watch or even to try to get Caleb to talk to him. He had been frightened when awakened by the bellowing below, but there was nothing which filled him with horror so much as the sight of Caleb in this condition. Just as before, he could not stay. So, easing himself carefully out of bed—as he might have, had he thought his brother was asleep—he tiptoed out of the room and down the stairs to Daisy.

CHAPTER

12

NEEDLESS to say, that night's scene did nothing to alleviate the increasing tension in the house. Though no one spoke about it, Saul was not the only one who had overheard the bellowing; nor was he the only one who knew what it was about.

The house was still most of the time except when Dora or Joanna decided to do something to attract attention or when May was home. She was the only one who, though aware of the situation, could forget it completely. She was so deeply buried in herself and in her Buddy that she had neither time nor thought for anybody else.

Saul, also, still had a good deal to say. But he did not say it at home; nor to the grown-ups who might tell his sisters or his mother. No, he talked to the other boys in the neighborhood; he couldn't resist telling them what a great man his brother was going to be. He didn't, of course, tell them about the white girl, but he talked incessantly about the time that was coming when there would be no difference at all between white and black.

He noticed, however—perhaps it was a week or maybe even a little less after that night of bellowing—that his audience seemed less eager to listen. They no longer yelled to him to come out, and when he went to find them, they had either gone somewhere or were called in by their mothers as soon as he appeared. It seemed strange; he could not quite understand. And if he had not been so angry, he would have been deeply hurt. Instead he was infuriated to see all the beautiful summer days passing in lonely boredom.

Saul was not the only one concerned by this either. Effie and Liza found the same situation when they went to the store. Usually the women on their front porches would wave and call to them as they passed. But now the porches were either empty or their occupants sewing too intently to see the sidewalk.

At the store, Jabez, who ordinarily asked after every member of the family—eager to discuss anything and every-thing—concentrated diligently on the cost of eggs and flour. He never joked about Saul's latest escapade or sent a lollipop home to Dora. He was all business, and his black eyes were cold as steel.

Even Ellen noticed the difference. At home a great deal since the birth of the baby, she missed the people that used to be always dropping by. She longed to see new faces and to talk to new people—even the neighbors would have been enough, and the days were long and empty without them.

Henry was, perhaps, even more concerned. Of course, he was at work all day and, therefore, did not have to contend with the cold back the world had turned on them constantly as his mother and sisters did. Still every evening when he went to Ruby's, he was tortured by fear and shame, wonder-ing always when her father would greet him at the front door with the suggestion that perhaps it would be better if he and Ruby did not see each other for a while.

Fortunately, however, that did not happen. Ruby was very much in love, and the Atwaters were kind. Of course, they could no longer boast of the fact that their daughter was practically engaged to one of the Blake boys. The news about Caleb had changed the position of that old and respected family considerably. It would, indeed, have been better, if possible, to hide Ruby's love for Henry. But as that was not possible, and as they were wise enough to see that only disaster could follow if the two were separated now, the Atwaters did not try.

Though Asa naturally had no problem like Henry's, he bore the chief brunt of Caleb's behavior. It seemed to him always that he was living a lie. Every day when Miss Elizabeth or Mr. Charles asked him about the children or how the new Sunday School building was progressing or whether he was glad Cameron Street had not been paved, he burned with shame as if he himself were committing a crime against them.

And this hurt even more because he was a Blake—born and bred in all the goodness and respect that name held. He remembered his father and his grandfather—a wizened black pygmy of a man with a shiny bald head and eyes too big for his emaciated face—talking about the days of the War when they had saved the old plantation house until the missus and the girls could get away to safety. Ever since then—and not just because of that, but because they were good, strong people with breeding—the name, Blake, had been one treated with respect.

Now he, oldest living bearer of the name, had produced a son who was trampling on the principles always synonymous with that name. But that was not the only reason for Asa's despair. He felt deeply Effie's faith and dependency in him; he knew she regarded him as the one person who could and would set things to rights. Therefore, he felt doubly discouraged and powerless each time he failed.

Yet Caleb was not even conscious of all the consequences his behavior could rain down upon his family. He was too involved with what he was doing, too concerned about his own situation on the other side of town to think of anything else. Things were not going as well there as they might. It seemed to him that the gathering at Roe's store was becoming more impatient every day, and he presided over each meeting wondering at just what moment they would rush up and tear him to pieces.

"Listen," Jake said one day. "It's two months since that law was passed. They ain't done nothin'. An' heah we sits twiddlin' our thumbs, waitin'. Caleb, you crazy if you think them white folks got it in they heads t' do somethin'. Ain't nothin' gonna happen 'less we does it ourselves. An' if you cain't do it, maybe we oughta get somebody will."

"Yeah. What we gonna do?" Hiram added. "All's we're gettin' now is poorer an' poorer."

Caleb knew that was true; he, himself, did not have a cent. Ever since quitting his job at the railroad, he had been living off the money the others could scrape together from their families. All the same, he pleaded, "Jes' wait till the schools open." He was becoming more uncertain of them every moment, and even as he talked, his eyes searched their faces uneasily. "Tha's only one mo' month," he continued. "An' then we got somethin' real t' fight fo'. . . . We get much furtha if we got somethin' definite."

They did not answer him. Some of them shook their heads and grumbled under their breath; they did not shout at him or throw him out. Apparently since he had been the original instigator and probably did understand the situation more thoroughly than any of them, they intended to go along with him as far as they could.

But Caleb's worries did not end there. He had another problem fully as harrowing as the situation at Roe's store. That was Trudy Reese—the white girl he had been taking out. She had never ceased to sicken him; indeed, as the ordeal stretched on from week to week, he found it harder—not easier—to see it through. Often when he started out to visit her, he felt himself nearly paralyzed with dread and disgust.

It was a winding, five-block walk from Roe's store to the

dirty white clapboard hovel in which she lived with her mother and her brother Billy, and every step of the way was agony. It was not Trudy alone who nauseated him so. He could not stand the sight of her large-eyed, shriveled, little mother. He knew every time he saw the overstuffed sofa that its gaudily flowered cover was crawling with vermin. And worst of all, he felt terrifying distrust for the brother.

Billy had yellow hair like Trudy's and he was tall with broad shoulders. But any claim which he might have had to good looks or even an appearance of virility ended there. For, his face was covered with pimples; his skin was a sickly yellow color. He emanated filthy indolence; his cruel, ice-blue eyes were the only part of him that ever seemed fully awake. They consistently regarded the world with a suspicious, sneering side glance.

Billy had never liked Caleb. Or at least he had never spoken to him, and Trudy said that was because of his dislike. At last, however, towards the end of July he did speak. He had been sitting on the curb, staring at the lumpy black tar which paved the street. But when he saw Caleb in the distance, he pulled himself up and went to meet him. His face was cruel and bitter, and he offered no greeting. He brought Caleb to a stop simply by standing menacingly in front of him.

"Listen, Sambo," he said, spitting the words out vehemently through thin, stiff lips. "We had about enough o' you 'round heah. Eitha you marry Trudy o' leave 'er alone. . . . I ain't right keen on havin' a black monkey in the fam'ly, but tha's bettah than the way things is now. Nobody else won't even lookit this house long as you come heah."

Caleb stared at the hard pimply face; for a moment he almost could not resist muttering a subservient "Yes sir" and skulking away. But at that point his fear of the crowd at Roe's store overcame that of the single yellow rat before him. Then he forgot fear altogether and remembered only the cause.

So, in the end he made no reply whatsoever to that pimply-faced muscleman. He just stood there glowering for a few minutes and then walked right on up the path to the tumble-down house. But ever afterwards he approached the place with shaking knees.

Of course, he told no one about this. He told the men at Roe's a version of what had passed between himself and Billy, but he never allowed them to see his fear. He had to hide that just to maintain their respect. And he could not tell the people at home anything either—not even the faithful Saul. He valued Saul's adoration too highly.

CHAPTER

13

*Y*ES, Caleb's behavior had played havoc with the life of the Blake family. But, though there was not one of them who did not feel sad, angry, afraid, though the worry about what new things he could be up to was always uppermost in their minds, the subject was carefully kept out of all conversations. Even Effie and Asa in trying to comfort each other did not dare to come right out and say what they meant. "Nevah min', Asa. Chillun has t' grow up of themselves." Or, "Y' know, Effie, he'll be awright; they always is"; but never any definite mention of Caleb. At the mere sound of his name, a conversation died and black eyes regarded each other furtively from under lowered lids.

Some three weeks after the news of Caleb's white girl, however, the whole affair suddenly burst into flames anew. It was Sunday. The sky was a pale, heat-glazed blue; the sun so hot that it had melted the tar on the streets. And the world was soundless, a vacuum from which every whisper had been sucked and in which even the hum of the locusts seemed only a vibration of silence.

All the Blakes—except for Caleb who was asleep—had been to church. But they had come home immediately after the sermon. Formerly they would have lingered to talk with their neighbors, but the experiences of the two preceding weeks had taught them the futility of that. The other churchgoers formed tight, fast-talking little groups. And when a Blake tried to work his way in, he was either ignored or, which was worse, the quick jabber gave way to painful silence. So, except for May who had stayed behind to talk to her Buddy, they had come directly back to the less strained atmosphere of home.

Effie and Liza went in to the kitchen to start dinner; Ellen went upstairs to change the baby. The rest sat on the porch and watched the parade of churchgoers on their way home. The monotonous buzzing which filled the air, the heavy sleepiness of the heat created a strange sense of peace in which it was almost possible to forget the family's disgrace and to think instead of the buttery, yellow corn on the cob and of the chicken frying in the kitchen.

Then suddenly the peace was shattered by a thunderbolt—a thunderbolt in the shape of May. Without any warning she came flying, stumbling through the hedge of the church-yard and across the hard-baked red clay. She dashed up the front steps—one hand already extended to grasp the door-knob. Her foot caught at the top, however, and instead of passing through the door, she collapsed into a sobbing heap on the floor. All of them—Asa, Henry and Saul—hurried toward her. But before they could get there, she had pulled herself to her feet again and run on into the house.

The screen door slammed behind her, and the three of them were left standing there paralyzed by silent horror. Though May was always noisy about both her happiness and her sadness, they had never witnessed such a violent scene as this one. What was more, they had never seen her unhappy when she did not throw herself upon someone, pour out her troubles, and ask for help.

Asa was the first to regain himself. "I'll go t' yo' ma," he said softly and walked quickly, quietly through the front hall toward the back of the house. He had no idea what to expect; his mind was imagining all kinds of things. But the one uppermost was a picture of May and her mother sobbing in each other's arms, and when he reached the kitchen, only Liza was there. Their eyes exchanged the looks of worry and sadness which they had exchanged very often of late. And, without being questioned, Liza said, "She went up t' May."

Asa went back to the hall and sat on the stairs. His face was ashen and drawn. He covered it with his long black fingers and shook his head back and forth despondently. He did not know what ailed May; he had no way whatsoever of even imagining it. But in those few minutes that he waited for Effie he felt as close to failure as he had ever been; he felt as if all his children were one by one being swallowed up by a horrible monster over which he was absolutely powerless.

Then Effie came. She sat down beside him and placed her large, capable but trembling hand on his knee. She turned her face towards him, silently pleading for help; he could see the fear and sadness in her deep dark eyes.

"It's Buddy," she said softly.

"What about 'im?"

"He say he ain't gonna see 'er no mo'. His fam'ly know 'bout Caleb; they won' let 'im."

Asa's whole body stiffened up. A tight knot formed in the pit of his stomach, and his head throbbed with a mixture of fear and anger. "Caleb's upstaihs," he said. "I could speak to 'im, but won't do no good."

"No. . . . Nevah min'. May fo'got he's home; I didn' tell 'er. It's bettah."

"Yeah. . . . Won't help nobody t' have a fight."

But they were wrong in thinking that May could satisfy her sorrow by merely sobbing it out. For, sorrow alone did not form the basis of her outburst; it was more than equaled by anger. And they were forced at dinner to undergo the very scene they had hoped to escape. It was the first meal

Caleb had eaten with the family in weeks. And—despite his behavior, despite the consequences which it had brought to their life—if May had been at the table, it would almost have been an occasion for celebration.

Instead they ate in silence, each from time to time casting stealthy glances at the empty place. Then suddenly there were footsteps on the stairs—sharp, clicking heels—and even before the sound had died away, May was in the doorway. She did not hesitate one second, but rushed immediately over to Caleb's place, screaming wildly at the top of her lungs.

"Damn you! God damn you! What you wanta do? Kill ever'body? . . . Sleepin' wid a dirty slut ever' night! P'radin' her roun' in cleah daylight!" Tears streamed down May's swollen face. Her little yellow hands formed two tight fists in which the knuckles showed white through thin skin. For a moment she had to struggle for her breath. But no one tried to interrupt; the silence was deadly.

"Well, you kin have yo' white gal. Only take 'er 'way f'om heah; take 'er wheah nobody kin see. Cain't anybody else have nothin' jes' 'cause you gotta have yo' white gal? Go 'way! Go 'way!! God damn you, go 'way! I'm gonna kill you if you don't."

All the time she was screaming, Caleb stared down at his plate, but as she said the last, he stood up calmly and struck her full force across the mouth. Instantly she was silent—right in the middle of a loud curse. Caleb swept swiftly past her and out of the room. In the stillness which he left behind, they heard the screen door slam.

Then May began to scream and sob all over again. She bewailed Caleb's behavior and pleaded with her parents to make him stop. And so dinner ended. Ellen, Liza, Henry and Saul just sat there in awful silence; little Dora even stopped beating her spoon against her glass while both Asa and Effie endeavored to calm May.

Eventually they were successful, or rather eventually she wore herself out. At last she sank into a chair and listened wearily to her father. His words were directed at her, but in reality they were intended for the whole family. And not one of them—unless it was May herself, exhausted by her tantrum—failed to catch the significance.

"Listen," he said. "Caleb's like the rest of us. Sometimes he do right; sometimes he do wrong. Maybe what he been doin' is wrong; maybe it do make people talk. But I'm the one handles that—not you. An' I don' evah want anybody t' talk 'bout Caleb again. I don' nevah, nevah wanta heah anotha word about it in dis house."

He never did either.

CHAPTER

14

O_F course, much as Saul hated it, July eventually stretched into August and August into September. That was not in reality the beginning of fall in Millboro. The days were still long, still weary and humming beneath a relentless sun. The leaves—except for those withered by the heat—remained a cool rich green. The birds still sang in the mornings—before it got too hot—and the crickets played on all night.

But officially it was fall. The season began with the opening of the schools, and this year the schools opened on the seventh of September. Liza said something about how foolish it all was and how impossible to get children to work in such weather. Saul did more than that. At least once a day from the twenty-fifth of August on, he kicked the side of the house and muttered a string of words which he had learned from Caleb and which his mother forbade him to use. But still the schools opened.

As it happened, however, things turned out better than Liza had anticipated. The authorities had been unable to complete a plan for the desegregation of the schools. (Some said they had not even tried and did not intend to.) Consequently the old policy held for another year. So, it was with much relief that Liza went back to her fifth grade. Saul, also, discovered that there were some pleasant aspects about school. It gave him a chance to be with boys his own age again. And he had sadly missed that during the summer.

For the others it mattered little whether it was August or September, whether the crickets continued their rasping nightly serenade or the birds flew south, whether the schools were open or closed. Nothing else changed. Henry and Asa still went to work every day, and May stayed with her job at the beauty salon.

But May was not at all her old self. She had never broken through the gloom which engulfed her after her scene with Caleb. She never went out, but even so, though she no longer had to rush through her meals, she still ate very little. She didn't even seem to care if she *was* skinny. Worse still, she never babbled or giggled about the obvious as she had before. And all of them, distracting as they had found that jabber, missed it now.

Especially Effie and Ellen who did not go out to work. The neighbor women who had once come daily to lose a few hours in cups of coffee, milk and sugar and meaningless chatter still pointedly stayed away. The days were long and silent and empty, the isolation almost unbearable. Often the two of them turned, exasperated, towards one another. But even then they said nothing. Only, "Did you finish that sock?" or, "I reckon it's most time t' feed the baby," or "Ain't it hot? You'd nevah know it was Septembah.' For, they could not speak of Caleb—the thing which weighed most on their minds. Every time the words pushed at their lips, they remembered what Asa had said and were silent.

And poor Caleb in his lonely world was having a harder time than any of them. Now that fall had come, now that the schools were open—and without putting the new desegregation law into effect—his previous means of control had slipped through his fingers. The others had lost all patience and, flinging caution to the winds, were champing at the bit for action. Caleb, angered to see that the authorities were daring enough to disregard the measure in this way, was equally anxious for action. But he wanted a bloodless, fool-proof plan, one which would bring results without thrusting them all into serious difficulties.

The others probably wanted that too. Though they talked a lot more, they would have been far less willing to give their lives for the cause than the quieter Caleb. They were just less patient, less particular. Roe alone stuck by Caleb. "Yeah, now's the time," he'd say. "But we gotta know what we doin' 'fore we do it. . . . White folks is jest as mad 'bout this as we is. Only they got the powah. . . . Don' fo'get, it's white folks makes the laws. We don' wanta jest end up in jail; ain't no good gonna come o' that. . . . We gotta think."

And so, because Roe, who was older and wiser, backed Caleb, the rest of them consented to go along. They really tried to think, too, as Roe had said they must, but always the plans they came up with were too wild.

Whenever Caleb suggested they wait and try to put their plea through when the state legislature came into session, they told him simply to shut up. Hiram wanted to go in a body to one of the white schools and force it out of session until colored children were allowed to enroll. Jake stuck by his old idea of going into movie theaters and restaurants armed and firing at those who tried to stop them. Even Jim Rogers—usually the silent one—said, "We waited long enough. It's fall like you said, an' I ain't waitin' no longah." He said it more than once too. But if they paid him any attention at all it was only to laugh. Jim was a sleepy boy, too lazy to walk, much less do anything else. It seemed quite obvious to all of them that he had only joined the crowd at Roe's as an excuse for quitting his job in the railroad yards. They considered his tone of feeble impatience as merely an attempt to keep his position in the rebellion secure.

After his scene with May, Caleb went home even less than

before. He spent his time drinking beer and playing poker (though not for money; none of them had money). Sometimes he slept at Jim's or Jake's, sometimes in the back of Roe's store. Every third night, according to his agreement with them, he went out with Trudy Reese. The result was that there were many nights when he did not go home at all.

Saul always worried when he woke up in the morning and found the pillow beside him as smooth as when he had gone to bed. But he never told anyone. His father had forbidden them to discuss Caleb; and even if he hadn't, the boy would have thought it disloyal to do so. At first he had talked about it at school. Not about the bad things like the white woman, of course, but about the good ones—how colored kids would be going to school with white kids, how colored people and white people would be able to eat in the hotels, sit in the same part of the bus, do everything the same. And, of course, he had made sure they knew Caleb was responsible for all that.

The other boys had seemed to like listening to this, they had crowded round him to hear more. And that was very pleasant for Saul after his long summer of loneliness. Within two weeks, however, the reverberations of his stories reached Asa. Then there was a long lecture before bed one night, and Saul was forbidden to ever talk like that again.

CHAPTER

15

ONE day—it was either the last week in September or the first in October—Liza was very late getting home from school. It was nearly five-thirty when she came plodding up Cameron Street, and Effie and Ellen were sitting on the front porch with the little girls, watching for her. "There she is," Effie cried, and little Dora, who looked up eagerly at her grandmother's words, started down the steps to meet her.

But Liza was not herself. She did not stoop to pick Dora up as the child had expected she would. She only looked down for a moment, said "Hello" and walked right on up to the porch. And even there she had little to say. Effie asked her to sit down a minute and rest with them, but she would not. "No, thanks, Ma," she said. "I'm goin' upstaihs; I have some papahs t' correc'."

"Aw, honey, you musta had a hahd day. Stop a minute."

"No. I wanta get it ovah with. . . . Call me when Papa comes home."

So up the stairs Liza went, but she was not able to keep her mind on the papers. Her thoughts kept wandering back to the scene in Mr. Jabez's store that afternoon. She could see it all clearly. The two men standing in front of the counter, talking in incredulous tones to Jabez. A newspaper was spread out before them and it was their disconnected readings that had first made her realize who and what they were talking about.

Her mind had frozen then with the terrible realization, and even now she found it difficult to believe. Difficult to believe not so much because of the person concerned, but rather because it seemed impossible that God could pour so much trouble on one family.

She tried to be reasonable; she attempted the plan she had always found most successful at times like this. What, she asked herself, what could it mean after all? Suppose what they said was true: Suppose Caleb *was* involved? Could anything so terrible happen? But the answer shot back quick and true— It would kill Mama. And so, even reason—Liza's most dependable defense—failed her in this case. At last she gave up even trying to correct the papers and just sat in the window watching for her father.

Meanwhile Saul, who had heard the same news—though through a different source—was just as quiet about it. They had come to him after school—the same boys who had listened with such fascination the weeks before when he talked to them about Caleb. But that afternoon they had not been fascinated. They had jeered at him; their faces had been angry and they had spoken with rasping voices. Then, when he tried to run away from them, they had screamed after him in cutting singsong words— "Yo' brotha's a murd'rah! Yo' brotha's a murd'rah!"— "Yo' brotha kilt a white man!" "Mistah Jabez say he'll get the 'lectric chair."

Saul had believed them, too. The words had struck deep and filled him with terror. He had never thought Caleb would go so far. But he did not try to argue with the truth as Liza did. He just ran home quickly to escape the words and the stones, should they follow. Then he stole in the back way and up the stairs to his room. He had vowed to himself that this was one secret he would not share with a living soul.

On the way home from work that evening Asa dropped Henry off at Ruby's. He did not wait for him; he was tired, and he knew that what Henry spoke of as a second might very easily turn into an hour once he saw Ruby. So, Asa left the boy and went on home.

No sooner had he parked the old Ford, however, and climbed out on the curb, than he saw Liza come running down the steps to meet him. Now, he knew Liza loved him, that she perhaps felt closer to him than to any other member of the family, that she was always glad to see him home. But the mere sight of her wiped away all the peace left in his heart by a day of hard work, just as one deep breath from a child can destroy a dandelion. Liza was not the type to come bounding down the stairs to meet him. Besides, the expression on her face was not a happy one. "Take me fo' a ride," she said to him softly as she came up. "Take me fo' a ride."

He looked down at her serious face and climbed back into the car. "We'll be back soon," he called to Effie on the porch; then he started the motor. Liza did not say a word for nearly three blocks, and then all she said was, "Let's drive out fahthah wheah we won't see anybody we know." After that she was silent again until Asa had driven outside the town limits where only clay hills and sleepy cows could see them. "Okay, Papa," she said softly. "You can stop now. I jes' wanta talk t' you; I heard somethin' at the sto' t'day."

Asa pulled the car over to the side of the road. "You don' have t' whispah," he reminded her. "Nobody's aroun'." But he knew, glancing again at the worried frown on her face, that she would whisper anyway. He bent his head low to listen. "What is it?" he asked.

She looked into his eyes and talked fast. Her face was still and anxious—listening for something; her long fingers gripped the edge of the threadbare seat. "I heard at th' sto'," she began, then ran out of breath and had to start again. "I heard at the sto' that a white man been kilt. . . . Stabbed. . . . Ovah cross town in that sto' belongs t' that friend o' Jabez's brotha. That sto' wheah they say Caleb goes. . . . It was in th' evenin' papah. An' Jabez tol' me—it's funny, he hasn't spoke t' me in weeks—he tol' me the man was de brotha o' the white girl Caleb been takin' out."

Asa looked at his daughter hard. He pulled himself slowly into a more erect position; every trace of life vanished from his usually strong, vibrant face. His eyes grew large, and the flesh hung loose from his great cheekbones. "I reckon it's true," he said at last. "I don' think Jabez'd make up somethin' like that. . . . He may not like you—Jabez—but he ain't mean." Then he hesitated again, looked out the front window at the dusty road ahead, and took a deep breath. "I wondah if they right," he said. "I wondah if Caleb really done it."

They sat there for a long time together, each silently trying to decide for himself what to believe. The sky turned misty blue and then gray. Finally Asa breathed a deep sigh, sat up straight, and turned on the ignition. They talked little on the way home, but they made one resolution: they would tell the others—all of them, even Saul and May—before the story came to them from someone else.

It was dark by the time they got back to Cameron Street. Neither of them spoke or moved for a moment after the car had come to a stop; they were both trying to assemble the words in their minds. But as soon as they had climbed the front steps, they realized that all their anxiety had been in vain. The whole family—except Caleb and Saul—was seated on the front porch, and they all of them—it was quite obvious because of the expressions on their faces—knew the terrible news. Henry, having heard it at the Atwaters', had returned home so upset that he could not keep it to himself.

Effie stood up as she saw Asa come up the path. But then her eyes met his, and she knew she need not talk to him after all. Therefore, she sat down again. Asa and Liza sat down too. Silence enwrapped them, and dark despair sat in every corner.

Only May could not be quiet. For a while she made a

valiant effort to keep her tongue in check. But at last she gave up, and the words rushed from her in a violent flood. "You reckon he really done it? . . . Listen, Papa, if he done it, you cain't let 'im come home. I ain't sleepin' in the house wid no murd'rah. Specially afta what he done t' me. . . . What you reckon they do t' him? You reckon they make us all go t' cou't? You reckon they 'lectrocute 'im? . . . Oh, Mama, I'm scared! I'm scared t' death! . . . I wouldn' even dare go t' work."

Nobody struggled to quiet her. But later when she had somewhat worn herself out and the rest of them had pulled themselves together a little, they talked the matter over. It was not a wordy conference; the cricket-throbbing silences took much more time than the actual talk. But they did decide a few things. As there was nothing they could do, they resolved not to try to do anything. They would just go on the same as ever, doing the same things they had always done.

Asa told May she must never again speak of her brother as she had. If he came home—guilty or not guilty—they would certainly take him in and be glad to help him if they could. And when it was all over, Effie said, glancing at the clock, "Oh, I do hope he comes home. I don' think he been back fo' two days now. . . . Oh, please, God, let 'im come home."

CHAPTER

16

E FFIE'S prayer was answered. Some time between ten-thirty and eleven o'clock that night, just as she and Asa were getting ready for bed, they heard the front door slam. Then, after a few moments of silence there were slow, heavy footsteps on the stairs. Effie pulled her ragged wrapper around her and started for the hall. She wanted to see her boy; she wanted to throw her arms around him; she wanted to ruffle his crinkly, short-cropped hair and ask him to tell her the truth.

There was almost a smile on her lips as she crossed the room. She turned the knob eagerly and pulled on the door. But it would not open. She tugged again impatiently, and then she saw that Asa's strong hand was braced against the top of it.

"That jes' make 'im mad," he said. "He don' wanta be babied. . . . Latah—aftah he's in bed—I'll go in an' talk to 'im."

Effie was disappointed, but she did not argue; she knew he was right. Turning away from the door, she picked up the trousers he had thrown over the back of a chair and hung them up in the closet. She turned down the bed and set the alarm clock for the next morning. Then the two of them just sat down and waited, eyes glued to the clock, for what might seem the proper amount of time to elapse.

Several times Effie looked over at Asa—her eyes dark and hollow—hoping that he might pat her hand or say something reassuring. But he did neither. Indeed, he did not even look at her. His eyes were far, far away, his forehead corrugated into tiny wrinkles, the rest of his face hard and anxious behind a restless hand. Asa was fighting inside himself. He was struggling to imagine just what mood he would have to deal with; he was searching for courage and the proper words. And he had a sinking feeling deep inside that neither would do him any good.

Asa need not have worried so, however. When Caleb shut the front door behind him and crept up the stairs, he had come to what he believed to be his last resort. He was tired —exhausted; his feet seemed to drag behind him. He was terrified—gaunt and shaking with fear. He had come home because that seemed like his one and only possibility for safety. But at the same time he knew inside that they could even get him here if they really wanted him.

He had been tortured so since one o'clock that afternoon, when he had first noticed the crowd surrounding Roe's store. Fear had not been the first thought to spring to his mind. Indeed, his first sensation had been one of pleasure. He had thought the people might be new recruits for the cause which the boys had rounded up. "We're doin' pretty damn good," he had thought and a tingling warmth had risen in his ears. He had started over towards the crowd, flaunting himself proudly, trying to attract due attention to his tall, powerful body. He reached the edge of the crowd and pushed his way in. He had to struggle to get through, and he told himself as he did so, "They don' know who I am. Else they'd make room. I'll tell 'em; I'll make a speech when I gets up theah." But when he *did* get there, when he *had* pushed his way through the crowd up to the very center of the room he did not say a word. He just stood there wide-eyed and stunned, while all the life and strength seeped rapidly out of him.

There before him, at his very feet, was Billy Reese. He was lying on his stomach with part of his pimply, sneering face turned towards Caleb and with the handle of a knife sticking up out of his back. No one had really seen Caleb—any more than he had seen anyone else. They were all too busy talking and conjecturing among themselves. But even so Caleb heard his name a million times as he forced his way out to the edge of the crowd again. And by the time he finally got there, he was—if possible—even more frightened than in that moment when he first looked down on the body.

Instinctively then, he ran with all his might, until he reached the vacant lot. There he sat down among the tall weeds and, in an effort to compose himself, searched for a course of action. He found great difficulty in doing that, however. His mind was so numb, so confused that he could hardly think at all. He knew—the idea pounded in his brain—that they were all thinking he had done it; they would tell each other that an argument had arisen between the two of them over Trudy and that Billy's death was the outcome. That seemed so logical—so very logical—that he began to believe it himself. The terror grew.

Suppose they found him; suppose they took him to jail; suppose the judge asked, "Did you kill Billy Reese?" What could he say? What could he possibly answer? He knew he had not killed Billy; he had not even known about it until he almost stepped on him there in the store. Still, it all seemed so logical. Could he have killed Billy without even knowing it—like the man in that story he had read who did all kinds of things in his sleep? Could you really kill a man in your sleep?

And, as unreasonable as that might seem, it was enough to convert his terror into blind panic. He felt like a trapped animal. He wanted to run—wildly, frantically, in any direction whatsoever. Yet, he could not move. His legs had turned into blocks of wood and would not obey his bidding.

He tried again to reason with himself. He must think of a place to hide. He could not go back to Roe's; that was certainly out. And the boys' houses? He could not go to any of them either; for, he knew there would be trouble after this. Chances were that none of them—even big-talking Jake—would take him in now. His mind fiddled for a moment over the idea of Jake. He wondered if Jake had killed Billy, if perhaps he had grown too impatient and done just anything to set off fireworks.

But he did not allow himself to linger long over that idea. There was no time to waste, and he turned quickly back to his search for a hiding place. For a moment he even considered trying to leave town. But he had no money, and besides it was too much of a risk; anyone would know him the minute they saw him. No, the only place to go was home. Perhaps that was not the safest place; perhaps, indeed, they would trace him there more quickly than anywhere else. They would take him handcuffed to the county jail, and within the week he would find himself headed for the electric chair. A little shiver ran down his back. His mouth puckered up as if he had just sucked a lemon, and tiny prickles of perspiration sprang up on his forehead.

Still, he had to go home. The police could pick him up anywhere if they had a mind to, and he felt he must go home once more before they did. He knew, at least, that after his recent scene with May his family would not ask questions. That made the prospect all the more inviting. Therefore— despite all the arguments which his reason could raise against it—he followed his heart and resolved to go home.

Even so he could not act upon his decision immediately. Though it might be inevitable that he would be caught, still he wanted to run as little risk as possible. So, he stayed in the vacant lot, lying as flat as he could among the weeds,

until it seemed dark and late enough for most people to be
at home. Then, because he was afraid of being seen on the
bus, he started walking. That was why it was so late when
he finally crept up the stairway to his room.

Saul was in there, of course. But because he was up gazing
out the window instead of being in bed, Caleb did not see
him. And Saul did not speak; he was too afraid. He did not
know whether the cruel words of the afternoon were true or
not. But he was terrified of saying the wrong thing.

Caleb pulled off his shoes and threw himself full-length
across the bed, one hand dangling loosely over the side. His
eyes closed immediately but he did not sleep. In a matter of
minutes his eyes were wide open again, shining in the darkness; his ears listened tensely for a siren in the distance or
heavy footsteps on the front porch. He dreaded the arrival
of the police. He knew they would come, but at the same
time, just as one departing on a long and perhaps heart-
rending trip wishes the train to depart as quickly as possible,
so he longed to get his own ordeal over with.

Saul's silhouette had disappeared from the window. As
there was no longer anything to watch for, he had slipped
down to the floor with his back to the wall. That seemed a
safer position, but, still in awe of his brother's gangling out-
line, he wondered with a fast-increasing terror just how long
it would take those eyes, burning in the darkness, to find him
in his corner.

Suddenly there was a knock at the door. Caleb started up
violently; his face was invisible, but the movement ex-
pressed terror. No second knock followed—only a momentary silence. Then the door was thrust open, and both boys
were able to distinguish their father in the coppery light from
the hallway.

Asa did not stand there long though. After a moment's
hesitation, he came quickly into the room and turned on
the ceiling light. His eyes, of course, fell on Caleb first, and

his mind fluttered in a final wave of panic before he chanced his dangerous undertaking. Then he caught sight of Saul under the window. "Son," he said, "go downstairs fo' a while. . . . Make yo'self a sandwich."

Saul did not stir. His teeth took a firm grip of each other inside the deceptive cover of his round, childish face. He did not want to leave; he wanted to stay and hear. He looked up at his father with large beseeching but uncertain eyes. Asa's stern black eyes returned his gaze. He had to look at the floor, and then he had to obey. In a single movement he sprang to his feet and disappeared through the door.

Asa did not look after him. His mind and his eyes were on his other son. Caleb was still sitting up. But his head was bowed; his arms hung limply from the shoulders; there was no expression on his face. Even his fear did not show. His brawny black figure seemed only a picture of overpowering dejection.

"Wanta talk t' you, Caleb," Asa began hesitantly.

There was no answer.

"Okay if I sit heah on de bed?"

"Sho."

A long expectant silence. Then— "Caleb, we . . . We heard some funny stories this aftahnoon. . . . Wondah—wondah was they true?"

Again no answer.

"Listen, Caleb, you mah boy—mah oldes' boy. I got a right t' know; it's my duty t' ask. . . . Caleb, I don' wanta hurt you; none of us does. We jes' wants t' help. . . . I wouldn' turn you in—nevah, no mattah what you done. . . . Makes no diff'rence. I'll do anything t' pertect you. . . . Jes' tell me the truth. Caleb, jes' tell me the truth."

Caleb continued to sit there in immovable silence, head bowed. But now his fists were clenched.

"That white man, Caleb? Was it you killed 'im? Was it you?"

Silence again, and then a slow, faltering, "No."

"You sure, Caleb? . . . Like I say, it don' make no diff'rence t' me. You mah boy; you mah pride, mah hope. I got faith in you, an' I wants you t' have anothah chance. I'd he'p you no mattah what. . . . But tell me the truth. Please tell me the truth."

"I tol' you the truth."

"It weren't you killed 'im?"

The veins bulged out on Caleb's neck. His head shot up like that of an excited race horse. "No, it weren't!" And this time the denial blurted out loud and hysterically.

"I'm glad, son," Asa replied in a tone exaggeratedly low and calm. "I'm awful glad." He put out his hand to touch Caleb's shoulder, and as he did so, the strong, hard figure collapsed into a sobbing, blubbering heap on the bed.

Like Saul, Asa was not only surprised but frightened by that. Then, after the first shock, he began to feel uneasy—almost embarrassed. He did not know what to do. He would have liked to bolt out of the room, back to the comfort and reassurance of Effie; still he did not move. After a few minutes he even sat down on the edge of the bed again with his hand resting on the great heaving body. He stayed there in the same position without saying a word until the sobs finally began to subside. Then, as the silence grew deeper, he turned out the light and tiptoed across the room.

"Good night, son," he said from the doorway. "Don' fo'get we on you side. . . . No mattah what happens, we heah."

It was very dark out in the hall after Caleb's door had been shut, and Asa found the silence deep and eerie. He hurried back to Effie.

CHAPTER

17

THAT marked the beginning of a terrible nightmare for the Blakes. Though, as Asa told them all, Caleb denied killing the white man, they did not know whether the police would believe him. Indeed, they did not even know whether to believe him themselves.

This did not, however, give them any uncertainty as to what they must do. They had made their resolution to carry on just as before, and they intended to keep it. That was the best way to prove to others that they had nothing to be ashamed of.

May was the only one who objected. "Please don' make me go t' work," she pleaded. "It'll give me the creeps. . . . All them white ladies lookin' me up an' down an' whisperin' 'bout me. They will, too; I know they will. . . . An' s'posin' they try t' make me talk? . . . Naw, I don' wanta go. Why cain't I jes' call up an' say I'm sick?"

She went though; all of them did except Saul, Saul who alone really longed to. He was eager to defend his brother's name against any of the other boys who might attack it. He had no fear of broken bones or a bloody nose. But Asa said, "You stay home in case yo' ma needs you." And Asa's word was law.

Yes, May *did* go to work. Where Asa's iron word might fail his iron will took over. Every day he drove May to work, giving her no chance to change her mind halfway there. He sat in the car and waited for her to go in. He did not trust her even that far.

But for once May was not just making up an excuse for not going to work. She was really afraid—mortally terrified all day long. Though in reality the slaying of Billy Reese was a story unknown among the white people of Millboro, though, indeed, even if it had been known, the clientele at Rose's Beauty Salon would never have thought to link it it with the skinny, honey-colored, little maid there, it seemed to May that both things were true.

Whenever they whispered, she knew it was about her being Caleb's sister; she never stopped to think that they would not have bothered to soften their voices to say anything they had to say about her. Whenever a new customer asked her name, she answered, "May," very quickly and sharply, quite certain within herself that they were really trying to find out her last name to see if the stories going around were true. Every afternoon she expected Miss Rose to call her to her desk and say, "I'm sorry, May, but because of what's happened I don't think I can keep you on here any longer." The thought of that made poor May prickle all over with humiliation.

And truthfully, she was not the only one who found it difficult to go to work. Henry had it easiest of all of them. His days were devoted to the solitary duties of mowing, weeding, hoeing; he never had to worry about relationships with either white or black. But Asa was as tortured as any man could be. When he sat alone with Martha in the kitchen—as he did a good deal of the time—there always seemed to be a tense silence. Martha was kind and civil; she had better sense than to speak to Asa about Caleb. But at the same time, agile talker that she was, she could think of no other subject for conversation. And Asa had no difficulty at all in seeing through the silence.

He found it even worse, however, driving Mr. Charles to the office or listening to Miss Elizabeth's orders for the day. It seemed unlikely that they would know of the trouble which had come to him, but all the same his heart jumped to double speed whenever they asked their usual questions about the family.

He felt like a traitor too. He had produced a son who was working against all the things these people believed in; his own flesh and blood was tramping down the power which kept him in food and overalls. He could never look Miss Elizabeth in the face any more; whenever she spoke to him his eyes were drawn, as if by magnets, to the floor. Like May, he wondered how long it would be before Miss Elizabeth told him and Henry she wouldn't need them any more. And worst of all, he could not have blamed her if she did.

Liza, however, was the only one who ran into concrete difficulties. She knew that Caleb's behavior had become the main subject of discussion in every Negro home. She knew also that the news of the killing had frightened many people; no one wanted trouble with the whites, and this was the very kind of thing that might bring it. She was afraid, therefore, on the first morning after the news had gotten out, of what her reception at the school might be. As she walked along, she even tried to think of answers should her pupils question her about the white man killed at Roe's.

But she was not in the least expecting what actually did happen. Indeed, by lunch time she had begun to hope there would be no real problem after all. Only one child had come to her desk at recess to ask what it meant for a colored man to kill a white man, and he had been quite satisfied with her curt, simplified answer. No further questions arose, and during the last half hour of the day, while the children did their addition of fractions on the blackboard, she told herself how foolish she had been to worry.

But her relief was premature. As soon as the bell had rung

and the last child run off at breakneck speed down the stairs, Mr. Lowell, the principal, sent for her. She quickly erased the blackboard—not bothering to wash it—jammed the rest of the papers into her notebook, and went downstairs.

Mr. Lowell was seated behind his desk; he rose nervously as she came in and remained standing until she had seated herself on the other chair beside his desk. He was a small yellow man with a balding head. His thin face was a cobweb of tiny wrinkles, and this afternoon the tracings on his broad, tight-skinned forehead had become deep puckers.

"Miss Blake," he began immediately, almost as if he were afraid the words might escape him if he gave them the chance. "I hope you won't find what I have t' say unreasonable. . . . I try t' be faih."

"Yes, Mistah Lowell."

His eyes studied the dirty piece of blotting paper on his desk. "As you know, since yestahday's trouble it's rumahed that yo' brotha was responsible."

"Yes suh."

"Mos' likely, they's nothin' to that rumah. . . . I remembah when Caleb was heah in school. He was a fine boy—intelligent, hahd-workin', eagah. . . . But still they's this rumah—"

"Yes suh."

"An' some people don' see things like I do, Miss Blake."

"No suh."

"Some people can make a lot o' trouble."

"Yes suh."

"So I have t' tell you I cain't keep you on heah jes' now. . . . It's not you, you undahstan'. It's only that folks are prejudiced. An' it ain't faih to children t' be kep' out o' school 'cause of somethin' they don't even know about."

"No suh."

"But soon's it's all ovah—even nex' week mebbe—you nevah know—but soon's it's all ovah, I be glad t' have you back."

"Thank you, suh." She stood up.

He stood up too. "I hope you undahstan' my position."

"Yes suh."

"I'll sen' you yo' check."

"Thank you, suh." And she was gone.

Actually it was just as well Liza was laid off. It meant, of course, less of the very necessary money coming in. But it meant also that Effie had someone to talk to. Ellen was far too preoccupied with the children to be any companion to her mother. And Saul certainly was of no use to anyone.

He sat on the front steps most of the day, staring bleakly at the empty, sun-baked street. Sometimes he threw sticks for Daisy to chase; sometimes he crawled under the porch for a nap; sometimes he even walked up the street to get something for his mother at Jabez's store. But no matter where he was, no matter what he did, he never shook off the solitary, defiant gloom which had become his master.

Sometimes he went up to his room, but the door was locked now, and he could only sit outside in the dark hall. Caleb would never open the door except for food or sometimes for his father.

Effie stayed downstairs. She cleaned vegetables and mended clothes; she cooked and scrubbed; sometimes she opened the Bible on the kitchen table and tried to follow with her finger the passages Asa had taught her to read. But they offered very little help. She was always tormented with worry; her wide-eyed silence was proof enough of that. She wondered what she must do if the police came and demanded to see Caleb. Sometimes she feared that all the neighbors, who had previously been such good friends, would start a riot or burn the house. Things like that had been done before. She knew; Caleb had told her once. None of these things happened now, of course, but that did nothing to reduce her fears. In her mind they were always just around the corner.

Caleb felt the same way. He never ventured out of the breathless attic room except to go to the toilet. And even then he tiptoed through the hall as fast as he could. All day he sat in the same position at the table in front of the window. He had a deck of cards and from time to time he played a game of solitaire. But mostly he just stared out the window, as if he could save himself if he caught sight of his pursuers before they saw him. And sometimes when he had become dizzy and half crazy with his endless watch, he would lie on the bed, face down in the mattress, struggling, struggling, struggling to make his mind be still.

Each moment seemed an eternity, and with each hour his terror grew an hundred fold. The strain and tension of waiting for something that never happened began to take their toll. Gradually his reason—the one thing on which he had always been able to rely—grew feeble. Though factually he knew he was innocent, his doubt grew stronger and stronger. By the end of the third day, he was almost convinced that he had killed Billy Reese. Death seemed his only real escape from agony, and he longed for it as does a man in excruciating pain. But at the same time, he prayed for just one more hour, even one more moment of safety.

CHAPTER

18

FIVE days went by in this way—though, of course, they seemed more like five years or five centuries. Then, on the evening of the fifth day the suspense was suddenly whisked away. It happened at about nine o'clock. They had finished supper nearly two hours before, and Henry, as usual, had gone immediately up the hill to see Ruby. The rest of them had straggled one by one out onto the front porch with the irresistible knowledge that it was fall and such evenings would soon be gone for another year.

The little girls had been put to bed, and for the first time in days Ellen sat with idle hands. So did Asa; he smoked his pipe and talked aimlessly with Effie while she shelled peas. Liza helped with quick, thin fingers which split each pod effortlessly, causing the peas to rain down in a steady plunk-plunk-plunk against the side of the wash tub. May just sat and watched; even she had nothing to say.

Saul was there too, but he was so quiet that he might as well not have been. He was sitting on the steps as usual—mostly just staring into the darkness, and sometimes, as if to get rid of unpleasant thoughts, rubbing his head against the thick hair on Daisy's neck. But all of a sudden his body jerked to attention. "Somebody's comin'," he blurted out. "They runnin'!" There was icy terror in his voice. What could it mean but trouble? No one had come to the house for days.

Effie dropped the peas, wash tub and all, as she peered anxiously into the darkness. Asa picked up his pipe and strode slowly, solemnly across the porch to the steps. And at the same moment Henry came bolting across the street, up the dirt path to the house. Even before he got there though, he bellowed—as Henry rarely did— "Hey, Pa. . . . Pa, I got somethin' t' tell you!" His voice was urgent; its tone gripped them with new fear.

But then he flopped down on the steps beside Saul and Daisy, and though his words jerked out squeeky and uneven because he was so out of breath, he told his news to all of them. "I was talkin' with Mistah Atwatah," he began. "When he come in f'om work, he say t' me, 'Lawd, Henry, I'm so glad t' heah the news! Tell yo' pa I'm mighty glad.' . . . Now I didn' know what in the worl' he was talkin' 'bout. So I was jes' fixin' to ask 'im when Miz Atwatah—"

"Yeah," Asa encouraged him. "What happen then?"

"Listen, Pa, anothah fella—Jim somebody—Jim Rogahs— admitted killin' that white guy. Some othahs seen 'im do it, an' they spoke up. The p'lice bullied ev'ybody, an' when they went fo' this Jim fellah, he had t' admit it. . . . Mistah Atwatah say they mos' likely only give 'im twenty yeahs or so 'cause it was mo' a fight than a killin'. Rogahs, he was kinda cut up, too."

For a moment they all stared silently at Henry. Then, in the darkness a sob escaped Effie's throat. Instantly Asa pulled a chair over and sat down beside her; he held her hand and stroked her shoulder. "Oh, I'm so happy, Asa," she kept sobbing over and over. "I'm so happy!"

The others said it too. Saul dragged Daisy to her feet and chased her round the yard. Ellen and Liza hugged each other. And May, of course, jabbered loudly to all of them. "Oh, I'm so happy!" she shrieked. "I was so scahed! . . . Oh, ain't it wondahful, Henry?! . . . Won't you scahed, Ellen?!"

But nobody answered her; she did not give them a chance;

besides they were too caught up in their own exclamations of joy. Then Asa, giving Effie's hand a final pat, stole silently in the front door. Henry was the first to notice he was gone; he grabbed Saul by the elbow. "Come on, boy," he grinned, "le's go down t' Mistah Jabez's. . . . We'll bring back ice cream—ice cream fo' ev'ybody."

Asa's cautious knock on the bedroom door was answered in the same suspicious and belligerent tone as always. "Who is it?" the voice asked.

"Pa."

"What you want?"

"I got somethin' t' tell you."

"What?"

"Lemme in first."

"Who's with you?"

"Nobody."

"You suah?"

"Suah."

"What you wanta tell me?"

"Lemme in."

The key turned in the lock. Slowly the door eased open a crack, and Caleb's bright eyes searched the darkness. Then he opened the door all the way. Asa went in. The door was shut again and locked, and the two of them stood face to face beneath the dull glow of the overhead light.

Caleb was the first to break the silence. "What you wanta tell me?" he asked.

"Come ovah an' set on the bed. . . . It's impohtant—what I got t' say."

Caleb obeyed, but as soon as he had sat down, he asked again, "What is it?"

"Fi'st I wanta talk t' you. I want you t' know that yo' ma an' me, we wanta help you all we can. Nobody come lookin' fo' you yet, but if they hada come we'd of hid you. Dat's true; Caleb, you b'lieve that's true?"

A short silence followed. Then— "Yeah, I b'lieve it."

"I'm glad; I hope you won't fo'git. . . . 'Cause . . . well. . . . Nobody ain't nevah comin' now. They found out who done it. . . . Somebody name o' Rogahs. . . . Jim Rogahs. You know 'im?"

Caleb's face jerked up suddenly; his eyes abandoned their study of the cracks in the floor. He was surprised that out of them all Jim Rogers had been the one to do it. "Yeah," he said softly, lowering his eyes to the floor again. "Yeah, I know 'im."

"Well, they got 'im. He admitted it."

Caleb said nothing, but the muscles in his face eased a little, and his eyes looked uncertainly into his father's, unyielding, determined to find the lie if there was one.

"Tha's why I wanta talk t' you," Asa continued. He did not give Caleb a chance to speak—or even to collect his thoughts. He knew that thought would only weaken his chances of success. So— "It's awright this time," he went on. "You got by okay. But nex' time might not be so lucky. . . . It ain't faih eithah, Caleb—the way you been actin'. We're a good fam'ly. We allus done what was right an' good; we allus been respected. Caleb, ain't faih fo' you t' ruin it."

Asa glanced furtively at his son out of the corners of his eyes. He saw the strong black body bristle with tension. But still he continued, knowing that now was his only chance to say what must be said. "Liza lost 'er job. . . . Buddy, he won't have nothin' t' do wid May. . . . Saul cain't even go t' school. . . . But that ain't what really mattahs; tha's all ovah with now. We wanta he'p you, Caleb; we wanta see you fin' the right road. . . . You cain't help b'lievin' what you b'lieve, but you gotta learn t' be patient an' wait. Long as you do that—long as you don' make trouble fo' nobody, we on yo' side."

Caleb said nothing, but now the anger was quite evident on his face.

"So," Asa dared to go on, "So, Caleb, you got anothah chance. If you want, I kin git Mistah Charles t' fin' you a job."

"I kin get my own job."

"Awright—if that's what you want, do it. It's up t' you." Asa tried not to sound demanding. He did not want to make the anger which he saw crouching in Caleb's face pounce on him with full strength. So he hesitated for a minute. But he could not stop; he had to go on. Even when he saw the fists draw together into two tight rocks, he had to go on. For, he knew what was not said then would never be said. "Awright," he continued, "Do what you want. . . . They's jest one thing I ask; they's jest one thing I won't stan' fo'. I don' nevah wanta heah 'bout you seein' no white gal—not evah again."

Caleb's lips grew thinner, but otherwise his face did not change. Nor did he speak.

"I cain't keep you from the otha side o' town," Asa added. "I don' like it—no; still, long's you got friends theah, I cain't do nothin' t' keep you away. . . . I mean that, Caleb, jest like it sounds. But if you evah go wi' that white gal again, I'd have t' stop you."

Caleb's silence made Asa uneasy; now he forgot about all he had said and wanted more than anything else to end his lecture on a happy note. The hard, bitter look on Caleb's face gave him little hope for that, but still he tried. He slapped the boy gently on the back and said, "Come on, Caleb. I reckon somebody went fo' ice cream by now. Come down an' have some with us."

Much to his surprise, the angry look slowly, hesitantly faded away, and Caleb, though with a voice still slightly sharp, said, "Thank y', Pa. I will."

CHAPTER

19

WHAT Caleb really intended to do, he did not really know himself. Such relief flowed into him at his father's news about Jim Rogers that he could not even think. Just hearing that someone else had been proven guilty gave him new peace and helped him to place more belief in the knowledge of his own innocence. He felt as if he had just lived through a wild storm, and nothing seemed so pleasant to him as the thought of just forgetting the last few months of his life and taking up the kind of existence led by his father and his brother.

Yet when his father suggested this, when he even dared to forbid the relationship with the white woman which Caleb himself had found so disgusting, anger and rebellion had surged anew inside him. He would have done anything—anything at all—just to prove himself master of his own life.

Fortunately, however, Asa had been wise enough to stop just in time. And his hand on the boy's shoulder, the kind smile on his face had persuaded Caleb to give in for a little while, to enjoy—just for tonight—the peace, the security, the love of home. He remained very quiet, however, and the worry about what step to take next would not leave him. Nevertheless, he followed his father down the stairs and took part in an evening which was the happiest one for the Blakes in a long time.

The weeks that followed, though, did not quite live up to the hopes and expectations of that night. Liza got her job back immediately. Mr. Lowell had been unable to find a regular replacement. Saul, too, returned to school, very eager, of course, to tell everybody about how his brother had been falsely accused of murder.

But other things could not be mended so easily. May could not go up to Buddy and say, "Look, it's all over. Take me back." Nor could they fly a flag from the house to show the world that all would be different now and to ask for their old respect back. Effie's worries about riots and police cars faded out completely, but there were still other things to be anxious about.

Though Caleb no longer seemed antagonistic, though he did not refuse to do as his father bade him, he was very silent. For the first week or so he stayed at home a good deal —sometimes sitting on the front steps or in the kitchen, but usually shut up in his own room. He seemed to be thinking very hard about something, something which he never mentioned to anyone.

Then gradually he began going out again, coming home later and later, and then not at all so that by the end of October the family suddenly realized that, unknown to them, he had slipped back into his old ways. They never spoke of it though. The barrenness which Caleb's behavior had brought to their lives had almost wiped away the memories of happier days. Besides, it seemed not only a dangerous subject but one on which little remained to be said. They watched, however, and their hearts formed cold tight knots in their empty insides. Asa's face was perpetually gray and drawn; Effie's eyes never lost their haunted fear.

It was a difficult decision for Caleb to make. He had enjoyed his week of security; it had been a great relief to know that no one was hunting for him, that no one could force him to do something dangerous or really wrong. But at the same time he had felt like a coward. He was taking the easy way out; he was doing what he wanted to do and letting the cause go to hell.

Yes, he began to feel guilty. Still—had it not been for Saul—he might even have been able to master the guilt. The boy was still fascinated by his older brother and the things he was doing. And as soon as the terrifying suspense was over, as soon as Caleb came out among them and left his door unlocked, Saul made use of every available opportunity to talk to him. He would sit down below him on the front steps with the pretext of petting Daisy; he would go into the bedroom to look for some paper or a pencil. And always he would end up asking, "Caleb, when you goin' back? . . . What they doin' now till you come back'? . . . Caleb, I tol' all the fellas at school what you doin'." Such constant reminders cut sharply into Caleb's conscience, and finally he was convinced that there was no alternative but to go back.

One morning he pulled on his overcoat and started out down Cameron Street to catch the bus. He felt troubled and uncertain, but at the same time, on the bus and later walking to Roe's store, his heart beat quickly at the prospect of seeing all the boys again. He was disappointed when he found only the storekeeper there.

Roe's eyes, set deep in his broad, fleshy face, opened wide with surprise. "Well," he said—his mouth curled into a crooked smile— "We didn' count on nevah seein' you again!"

"I couldn' come; I had t' lay low."

"Yeah. Guess you was scahed. They was aftah you at first."

"They really thought I done it?"

"Yeah."

"Who tol' 'em I didn'?"

"Me. . . . Me an' that white gal you was goin' wid . . . his sistah. . . . She tol' 'em."

"Oh. . . . How come they got Jim?"

"He turnt 'imself in; he was scahed. . . . He's gonna get it, too. Wouldn' be s'prised if they give 'im twenty yeahs."

"Yeah. Po' Jim. I nevah woulda thought o' him. . . . They done anything while I was gone?"

"Not much. . . . I think they kinda scahed. . . . They have a coupla meetin's, but 'tain't much 'thout you. . . . You comin' back, Caleb?"

"I reckon so."

"Good. . . . It'll be bettah. . . . I think they learnt they lesson."

After that Caleb went every day. They gladly took him back, and all of them—even the action-seeking Jake—promised to do whatever he asked. At first everything moved slowly and smoothly. But before long, indeed, in less than a month the men had resumed their old ways. The demands for action came with new frequency and strength. Lots were drawn, and several of the men—Caleb included—were forced to go with white girls.

Caleb resumed his relationship with Trudy with much misgiving. She treated him no differently because of her brother's death; indeed, that seemed to have made little impression on her. She only remembered it—as she did all other things—when it could be useful to her. She must have thought it a good weapon against Caleb. She made it quite plain that she felt she had a right to him now.

But Trudy did not know Caleb. Bluntly as she might state her claim to him, her meaning did not penetrate. He felt only two emotions toward her—disgust (perhaps even more than before) and hatred because she was so willing to forget her dead brother and come back to him. But even worse than these two which tore and gnawed at his insides whenever he was with Trudy was the cold, unearthly silence which seized his brain sometimes when he was sitting next to her and even at times when he was alone, walking home in the terrible darkness that comes before dawn.

Asa's voice came to Caleb clearly out of that silence, and he found it impossible to brush away his memory of the kind but unyielding expression on that strong, black face. The voice said over and over—gently but clearly, too, and with great determination, "They's jest one thing I won't stan' fo'. I don' nevah wanta see you wid a white gal again."

Unfortunately, though, that was only a memory. It could be drowned out by the loud and insistent demands of the fellows at Roe's store. Caleb kept on seeing Trudy.

But somehow—probably because they did not want to— Asa and Effie did not discover this immediately. They knew he was out a lot and came home very late. Also they knew better than to expect him to give up his friends and his hangouts across town. He did come home for supper two or three nights a week, and they tried to persuade themselves that a fair part of his time was spent in job hunting. Once, indeed, after several weeks had passed, Asa asked if he had found work yet. But even when the blunt, offended "Nope" came back at them, he and Effie refused to be discouraged.

It was not until well into November that they found it impossible to evade the truth any longer.

CHAPTER

20

EVEN then things might have run on as before. None of them were out looking for trouble; all of them would have been thankful for the peace and security of a happy ending. But Caleb thoughtlessly allowed things to go too far. He felt troubled about having rejected his father's advice and stamping down his ideals. But at the same time, buried as he was in worries about Trudy and how long the men would hold out before something else like the murder of Billy Reese occurred, he forgot, almost completely, about the people at home.

He forgot and, therefore, when he was very tired or when it was exceptionally late, he would just lie down on a couch at Roe's or Jake's or anybody's and sleep without going home at all. He hardly even realized it when five whole days went by in the middle of November without his once setting foot on Cameron Street.

It was too cold then to sit on the porch any more. Even Daisy, whose tongue had hung out pitifully all summer, preferred to lie in the kitchen near the stove. And the rest of them followed her example. There was, of course, heat in all the other rooms, and besides Asa built a fire in the parlor twice a day—once before he left in the morning and again when he came in at night. But the kitchen always seemed cozier, and the parlor was never used at all except in the evenings when Effie refused to have them all underfoot while she was cooking supper.

Winter is often the warmest, closest, sweetest time of year, and so it had always been with the Blakes. Of course, there was rarely the snow and ice which Saul read about in books at school, but it was still cold enough to make people stay near home. Usually there were neighbors who came in of a winter evening. They would bring cookies or doughnuts, and Effie would make a pot of cocoa. They would just sit around and talk until bedtime.

This winter, however, there were no such visitors. Sometimes Ruby Atwater came over, but more often Henry went to her house. The evenings seemed as long and empty as the days. And probably it was this loneliness more than anything else which drew attention to Caleb's absence. Undoubtedly, had it been July when they could sit outside and watch the passers-by or the people in the next yard, they would scarcely have noticed that Caleb was not there. But now when there were no visitors and when the family was so closely cooped together, he was easily missed.

Besides, though Effie and Asa had become used to his irregular hours, when he began staying out all night, they could not overlook it any longer. One night Asa came home to discover that for the third day in a row Caleb had not been home. Effie knew by the hardness of his jaw and the pucker between his eyes that he would not be able to go along with it much longer. "He didn' come home 't all?" he asked her.

"Naw, an' I kep' the pot o' soup on the stove all day, ready t' heat fo' 'im. . . . I ask Saul too; even he ain't seen 'im." Effie looked up cautiously from the sock she was darning as she said that.

Asa shook his head disconsolately. But there was more than sadness in his face; there was something like anger too. Effie saw it, and she shifted her eyes quickly back to her work. "I warned him, Effie," his forlorn voice droned. "We gotta give 'im time, but this cain't go on fo'evah."

Effie did not answer. She knew better than to interfere or ask questions. The handling of these problems was Asa's duty.

The next evening when he came home Asa did not even ask about Caleb. His eyes searched Effie's, saw their emptiness and knew. By the fifth night he did not even have to see Effie to know the answer. He had found Saul on his knees before the front window. His elbows had been braced against the sill, and his nose pressed in a cloud of mist against the glass; he did not even turn to look when his father slammed the front door.

Asa headed straight for the kitchen, but he did not find Effie there. With considerable effort Ellen had at last managed to get her to take a rest in the parlor. He went back and found her there with Liza and the two little girls.

Liza got up from the papers she was correcting and came across the room to kiss him. "Evenin', Papa," she said.

"Evenin', honey." But he only kissed her forehead absent-mindedly and then walked blindly past little Dora who came running up to him with outspread arms. He went over to Effie's chair beside the fire and put his strong hand on her shoulder. "Evenin', Effie."

"Evenin', Asa. . . . He ain't been home."

"Naw. . . . I seen 'im t'day. He won' be comin' home."

"You seen 'im? . . . Wheah you seen 'im? What you mean he ain't comin' home?" Her voice was close to frenzy; tears pushed at her eyelids.

But, though he realized this, Asa's tone was no gentler than before. "Yeah, I seen 'im." And he said it definitely, deliberately—to be sure that he understood as well as Effie.

Effie did not speak again. Just the tone of her husband's

voice was enough to reveal his intentions, but she knew better than to interfere. Instinct told her to plead with Asa, to grab hold of his arms, to shake him, anything at all to keep him there beside her. But her experience checked all these impulses; though she knew he would not stay anyway, she was not even permitted to intervene. And only when he had turned to go did she manage to say, "Please, Asa, don' do nothin' you be sorry fo'."

That was ignored. "I'm goin' out, Effie," he said. "Won't be heah fo' suppah."

"Yes, Asa."

"Good-bye."

"Good-bye, Asa." There were tears on her cheeks, and it took all her self-control not to reach for his hand. He kissed her and went back out into the hall, while the rest of them stared after him in silence.

Liza, perhaps, saw something strange in her father's behavior, but only Effie knew what that strangeness meant, and she was praying with all her heart that she might be wrong. She heard the cellar door, just as she had expected. And then she called Saul into the parlor—that part of it was her duty—so that he might not see Asa on his way out. The boy came obediently, happy despite himself to be distracted from his hopeless vigil at the window. He lay down on the floor near the fire and rubbed his hand along Daisy's head.

Effie heard the cellar door shut again. Her hand, still holding the needle, stiffened, and her lips formed a thin tight line. But she said nothing. Then the front door shut, too.

"Wheah's Pa goin'?" Saul raised his head quickly.

"I don' know."

"Didn' he tell you?"

"No. An' if he did, it's none o' yo' business."

"I'm sorry. . . . It's jes' kinda funny he didn' tell you."

Liza interrupted then. "Saul, go see if you can help Ellen wid suppah. May's upstaihs, an' I gotta finish these papahs."

Meanwhile Asa had driven the rickety old Ford downtown to the middle of Main Street. It was difficult—though he had planned his strategy earlier—to leave the car there and walk the rest of the way. For, when he reached over into the back seat and felt the cold hard barrel of the gun in his hand, he wanted to turn right around and go home. He remembered the look in Effie's eyes; he heard her say, "Please, Asa, don' do nothin' you be sorry fo'." His eyes grew moist, and he could feel his will power melting away.

"But I told 'im," he reminded himself. "I wahned 'im time an' again."

"Yeah—but he's so young; Effie love 'im so much."

"He ruint his fam'ly though, an' when he got anothah chance, he ruint it again. . . . It's mah duty." And he knew it was his duty. He could remember how—when he was a little boy—it was rumored that Jake White had shot his son. Asa's father had tried to explain it to him. "It was his right, son," he had said. "It was his duty. You gotta give people plenty o' chance. . . . But when they don' pay any heed, when they go right on hurtin' people, it's yo' duty. You ain't got no choice." At the time and for years afterwards Asa had not agreed with his father. But now when the duty was his own, he realized the full weight and meaning of it.

Reluctantly he climbed out of the car. He placed the shotgun next to his body and pulled his overcoat tightly around it. "At least," he reminded himself—and it was a consolation— "At least I won't be doin' it in anger." But at the same time he was almost sorry about that. Anger might cause remorse later; but now it would have gotten the job over quicker and more easily.

He walked down the street as briskly as possible with the end of the gun bumping against his legs. An increasing panic inside told him that if the job was not done now it never would be. Besides, he was convinced that even in the darkness the few people he passed could see the bulging of the gun under his coat.

He went directly to Roe's, but when he got there, he didn't go in. He just looked in from the street, his face so close against the window that the glass grew steamy with his breath. There was a crowd inside—people at the tables, leaning over the counter, just standing around. Most of them were drinking; their voices were loud and raucous. Asa squinted and looked hard for Caleb. He searched again and still again. Then his heart began to throb with joy. Caleb was not there. His body relaxed into almost hysterical relief, and after glancing upward once more at the sign over the door, he started back towards Main Street.

As he turned the corner, however, he stopped dead. His knees shook; his face—even in the cold—became beaded with perspiration; little shivers ran up and down his back. He could not understand at first why he felt that way. All he saw was a couple walking slowly down the street in his direction. At first, when he saw the girl's hair turn to silver gold under a street lamp, he thought he was just surprised to find a white couple walking in that neighborhood at night. But then, he noticed something familiar about the man. And it was in that instant that the cold terror seized his heart. He edged over behind the shelter of a tree trunk. He stood motionless for a moment there and squinted at the approaching couple. Then he slowly raised the gun and took aim.

As he did so, Asa remembered all the hopes he had had for this boy and all the things he loved in him—the warmth he had shown as a child, his pride in joining the church, his determination in all he undertook. Sweet things too—the way Caleb slapped his knee in excitement, the strong, good handshake he had, the way his eyelids still lowered when Effie kissed him.

But even as these thoughts ran through Asa's mind, his finger grew tense. It hesitated for a moment in iron fear and then released the trigger. Asa heard the click and then the scream, but he did not look to see if the load had hit home. There was no need for that. Asa had hunted ever since he was a boy; he never failed to hit his mark.

CHAPTER

21

*I*T was almost ten o'clock when the Ford drew up in front of the house again. Saul had been sitting before the window all evening; a thousand times he had mumbled to himself or to anyone on hand, "Wondah wheah Pa went?" Now, at the sight of the car, he screamed at the top of his lungs, "Hey, Mama, Pa's home." Then he flung open the front door. And, though the cold wind cut into him and raised thousands of little goose pimples, nothing could draw him from the spot.

Effie called to him to shut the door and come into the parlor. He paid no attention the first time, and when she called again, he did shut the door but still could not tear himself away from the window. Frightened, she rushed out to make him obey but by that time it was too late. Asa was already coming in the door; his shotgun was in plain sight under his arm.

"Wheah you been, Pa?" Saul asked. But Asa's face was serious, the muscles around his eyes tight, his lips gray. He did not answer Saul or even speak to Effie. He just walked straight past them toward the cellar door. Saul said nothing in his absence; instead he searched his mother's face anxiously, trying to find the answer there. When Asa came back, his coat was unbuttoned and he no longer had the gun.

"I got some suppah on the stove fo' you, honey," Effie said.

"I don' reckon I'll have suppah," his voice dragged wearily. "I'm tihad. Reckon I'll go t' bed."

Saul's curiosity could be quieted no longer. "Nevah knew you t' stay out so late, Pa," he hinted.

"Saul, you go t' bed. An' min' yo' own business. Yo' pa's too tihad t' be pestahed."

"Okay. G'night." He was angry; anyone would have known it by the slow, silent way he climbed the stairs. But neither of his parents tried to reason with him. They only held their tongues and waited until he had disappeared around the bend in the stairs.

Even then they did not mention what was uppermost in their minds. Effie spoke again of the supper on the stove, and this time Asa agreed. He felt, as he knew Effie did, that they must stay together now.

The kitchen seemed much warmer than the hallway. The ceiling light was on, and a faint aroma of warm food came from the stove. Effie took a steaming plate from the oven and set it before her husband. Then she sat down at the other end of the table.

Asa ate in silence. He cut the ham methodically into large chunks and carried each forkful wearily to his mouth. His face was dead and hollow-eyed. The only parts of it which moved were his jaws, and even those gnawed so slowly, so slightly that the motion was hardly visible.

Effie did not bother to ask if he had accomplished what he had set out to do; she did not need to. And, for once, she had lost control of her emotions. A tear slid slowly down the full curve of one cheek. Another followed and then another. They made shiny, wet paths to her chin where they either dripped off or were wiped away. But no sound escaped her partially open lips, and though Asa was aware of her tears, he did not try to comfort her. He knew that he could not, and he knew, too, that she did not expect it—no more than he would have expected her to reproach him.

So, even after Asa had finished eating, they sat on there in silence. They listened to the hollow ticking of the old clock and to the plunk-plunk of rain on the tin roof. Somewhere —far away—a siren whistled feebly through the night for a moment and was silent. In that moment a tiny pucker appeared in Asa's forehead, and terror lit Effie's eyes. But then, as the silence returned, they relaxed into a somewhat relieved but still anxious listening.

They were waiting—for what, they could not be certain, but for something—definitely for something. Their hearts beat rapidly in the suspense. And had it not been for their sorrow, fear might have taken over with full strength.

It was not late—only a little after eleven—when the knock came on the door. Effie's eyes opened wide; a tear stopped midway down one cheek. She did not get up immediately; she was too afraid. And though she knew hesitation would do more harm than good, though she knew whoever it was at the door would still be there no matter how long she waited, she sat frozen in her chair.

There were three more loud knocks before she finally reached the door. Effie held her breath and undid the latch. She tried valiantly to raise her eyes from the floor and meet the gaze of the men facing her. But from that moment self-composure was next to impossible. For, there on the porch —looking at her solemn-eyed out of the darkness—were Jabez and Frank Atwater—two of the many people who had not come near the house for months. And behind them—though the street light which lit the scene was 'way down at the corner—Effie could see many, many dark faces.

"Y-yes, yes," she stammered. "C-c-come on in."

"Effie, we got somethin' t' tell you. . . . Somethin'—"

"C-c-come on in then. Come in out the cold."

They hesitated for a moment, hovering like a storm cloud. Then somebody else pushed his way to the door. It was Henry. "Ma," he gasped. His eyes were wild, his face hurt and afraid. His lips were thin and gray, and the words bolted out of them like runaway horses. "Ma. It's Caleb. Somebody kilt Caleb. They bringin' him home."

This was, of course, no shock to Effie. The shock and pain had struck much earlier that evening; they had since become only a gnawing, aching emptiness. Besides, she was not much of an actress. Lying had never come easily for her, and it took all her strength now to attain any deception whatsoever. She gave Henry's cold hand a hard squeeze and looked deep into his eyes. Then she turned to the others. "Well, bring 'im in then," she said softly. "Bring 'im in."

Those in the front shifted aside a little to let the four men carrying Caleb pass through the door. "Where'll we put 'im?" Roe asked.

Effie didn't know it was Roe. She didn't know most of the men at her house that night. She only knew there were more people than she had seen for a long time. She did not answer Roe's question immediately; she had not even heard it. Here was her boy—her tall, strong boy—borne home limp and bloody, gray-faced and silent by roughnecks she had never thought he would even set eyes on.

"Where'll we put 'im, ma'm?" Roe asked again.

"He ain't so light, y' know," another put in.

"Oh!" Her mind snapped back to his words. "Upstaihs, I reckon. . . . Yeah, upstaihs. You show 'em, Henry."

Henry stepped ahead, and the four of them followed him. They watched their feet carefully as they climbed the dark stairway. Effie turned back to the other men who were waiting half inside the door and half still out on the porch. Her mind spun around in its effort to choose a course of action. She took a step closer to Jabez and Frank Atwater; they were the only two she could recognize out of the darkness and her own confusion. Then she said, "Wait. Lemme call Asa."

Awakened by the noise, Saul had crept out into the upstairs hall; he had thought, at first, that it might be one of the riots he had heard May talk about. Then when he saw the four men carry Caleb, bloody-faced and limp, up the stairs and past him to the spare room, he had decided he could not stay up there any longer. Therefore, when Effie turned to go after Asa, she suddenly found Saul there beside her. The sight of him surprised and frightened her momentarily; still she managed to act reasonable. "Saul," she said, almost as if she had known he was there all the while, "go get yo' fathah."

The boy turned instantly, and it did not take him long to accomplish his mission. When he got to the kitchen doorway, he found his father already standing there. Asa's face was twisted by sadness and fear; instantly as Saul saw it, the memory of the shotgun flashed across his mind, and he knew the truth. He could not understand it, of course; it seemed unreal, something that could happen only in a terrible nightmare. In that moment of recognition, the boy felt a wild revulsion for his father; had he had a weapon, he would have used it. But then as the full meaning of the hollow bleakness on his father's face came through to him, both fear and hatred collapsed. They gave way first to confusion, then to something very close to understanding. "A lot o' men out theah, Pa," he said. "They brought Caleb home."

Asa saw the horror and the pain and the confusion in the boy's eyes, but he did not have the strength to pat his shoulder or to squeeze his arm. He had all he could do to control his own emotions and to face the ordeal ahead. Without a word, he stepped quickly past Saul and through the doorway to the hall.

They were all silent when he appeared. He walked slowly to stand beside Effie and put his hand on her shoulder. Each man there watched this and saw the heavy, back-breaking despair which had settled upon him; each marveled that a man could age so suddenly. The silence was tense; Jabez and Frank Atwater exchanged anxious glances. At last Jabez stepped forward. "Asa," he said. His tone was gentle as one you might use in addressing a sick child. "We brung Caleb home. . . . He's . . . He . . . Somebody . . . He was killed. They found 'im in the street; won't nobody in sight. . . . Ovah theah they think a white guy done it. That case, ain't no use t' get the police. They only make trouble in things like this."

The whole time Jabez was speaking, Asa's head was bowed in apparent study of the floor; nor did he look up in the silence that followed. Even when he replied it was without any expression; indeed, with hardly a movement of his lips. "Thank ya, Jabez," he said. "Thank you all." Then he turned around and went back to the kitchen.

The crowd shifted restlessly from one foot to the other, uncertain as to whether this was the end or not. Then it separated itself into little groups which dispersed into the night. Finally only Jabez and Frank Atwater remained. They refused to come in when Effie asked them. It was late, they excused themselves, and besides they knew she and Asa would want to be alone together at a time like this.

"But," Frank added—and it seemed to Effie there was more than kindness in his face, more than sympathy, something you might almost call respect. "If you want anythin', if they's anythin' we can do t' help, jes' send us word. . . . Asa looks kinda cut up." His eyes fell to the floor quickly. "Takes a lot o' courage fo' that, Effie. I couldna done it."

"Me neitha," Jabez mumbled.

The silence that followed was heavy and uneasy. In an effort to dispense with it Frank Atwater ventured clumsily onward, "Ruby an' Tildy be ovah t'morrow. But if you need us meantime, jes' send Saul."

"Same heah, Effie. . . . I'll come the minute you say."

"Thank ya," she replied simply. "We're grateful." Her

eyes still avoided theirs in an endless study of the floorboards.

"Good night," Frank said. And Jabez echoed, "Good night, Effie."

"Good night." And as they started down the path, she mumbled under her breath, "Thank y' very much." She stood there for a long time. The two men disappeared into the night; the cold dampness brought little goose pimples out on her arms. But still she did not move—not until the hall light was suddenly snapped out. Asa shut the front door gently. Then together they climbed the dark stairway.